THE JUDGEMENT OF
THE SEA

FOUR NOVELLAS
by Gertrud von LeFort

INTRODUCTION
by Karl Stern

Translated by Isabel and Florence McHugh

HENRY REGNERY COMPANY
CHICAGO • 1962

This book is a translation of the four short novels entitled *Das Gericht des Meeres, Am Tor des Himmels, Plus Ultra,* and *Der Turm der Bestaendigkeit* originally published by Insel-Verlag, Wiesbaden, Germany.

ACKNOWLEDGEMENTS

The HENRY REGNERY COMPANY gratefully acknowledges the assistance of Ursula Feldmann whose precise understanding of Baroness von LeFort's wishes for this translation have made possible its publication.

172891

CONTENTS

INTRODUCTION

THE relationship of German literature to the world outside is a dark and bewildering chapter. Although
statistics are not available, I have no doubt that in Germany
they perform more Shakespeare, Shaw and Wilde than in
England, more O'Neill than in America, and at least as
much Molière as in France. When we were schoolchildren
we became as saturated with Shakespeare in the translations
by Tieck and Schlegel as English schoolchildren become
with the originals. *"Sein oder Nichsein, das ist hier die
Frage"* is a proverbial saying which, in the usage of generations has shed its quotation marks—so much so that, when
some years ago an old school friend of mine from Munich
days and I were sitting in a Montreal movie house listening
to Laurence Olivier's *"To be or not to be, that is the question,"* my friend nudged me and whispered: "Excellent
translation!"

The trouble is that all this has been a one-way traffic. In
the twenty-five years I have been away from Germany I
recall exactly two performances of German plays in English

(one was an adaptation of Schiller's *Mary Stuart* on Broadway, another was Kleist's *Broken Jug* in Stratford, Ontario). The situation is no better in fiction. I remember how surprised I was when Somerset Maugham mentioned among the dozen or so best novels of world literature Goethe's *Wilhelm Meister*. By that time I could not imagine that anyone outside Germany, except professors in German departments, had ever heard of this book, let alone read it. To be sure, there are exceptions—Rilke, Mann, Kafka and Brecht—but it is hard to say how much of this is mere snob appeal. (In the first mentioned, at least, there is much circumstantial evidence to justify the suspicion.)

This is not the place to discuss the reasons for all this. Suffice it to say that an evil fairy has made the best fruit of German letters unexportable, and has allowed a good deal of contaminated seed (e.g. Hegelian dialetics in the guise of Marxism and Fascism, the worst of Nietzsche etc.) to slip through the customs.

The case of Gertrud von LeFort is quite particular. Her work deals—as far as one can summarize it at all—with the Mystical Body, the hidden Church and the Church in history, and the mystery of womanhood. These themes are, by their very nature, interwoven. And they ask, also by their very nature, for a treatment in *chiaroscuro*. Hence, Gertrud von LeFort's style seems always to be that of legend and chronicle, even when she treats contemporary themes. That legendary style is the trickiest of all literary devices. It creates a subtle interplay between history and myth, between the realistic and the symbolic. There are few writers who get away with it (think of all the false Victorian tales of the "quoth he" variety!). Among the few who did succeed, however, we find a surprising number of women: Selma Lagerlof, Sigrid Undset, Isak Dinesen and Gertrud von LeFort. This is no coincidence. Dusk, the twilight between dream and reality, is the world of tales told by mothers. The German language has an intranslatable verb—*raunen*. It means *to murmur, to whisper,* but it is also related to *rune,* and often used with an archaic flavor in connection with the telling of tales. The legendary tone is that of the *raunen* of women, the murmur in which past and future blend, the tone of chronicles and Sybyl. "The core of the feminine mind," says Otega y Gasset, "no matter how intelligent the woman may be, is occupied by an irrational power." Of course, "irrational" in this connection does not mean "foolish" or "unrealistic." The better word would be "transrational." In the stories presented here we notice that the stronger the imagery is, the more it eludes discursive interpretation. Take, for example, *The Judgement of the Sea*—Motherhood and the Sea and Sleep and Death and Eros—the symbols are all interrelated but in the way of the dream. They owe their poetic energy precisely to the fact that they cannot be reduced to a thesis. We have entered *das Reich der Mutter,* the mothers' orb.

The air of remoteness is deceptive. Indeed, Gertrud von LeFort's preoccupations are too timely for comfort. Before the German cataclysm she dealt with the drama of Synagogue and Church (in *The Pope of the Ghetto*); quite early she touched, at least tangentially, on the ecumenical question (in *A Wedding in Magdeburg*). In *The Song of the Scaffold,* of course, she dealt with the hidden cross of anxiety in a manner which today many people would fatuously call "existentialist" and in her best known work of non-fiction, *The Eternal Woman,* she examines some of the most burning problems of present-day actuality in a way which is strikingly direct and original.

What we said in the beginning about the one-way traffic of German letters refers also to "Catholic literature." (One needs plenty of inverted commas here, since the term is, at best, doubtful.) Why have Graham Greene and Francois Mauriac had a world-wide impact, while few people outside Germany have heard of Gertrud von LeFort and nobody ever of Reinhold Schneider? The reason cannot be that of artistic competence. With all our admiration for Greene's genius we must admit that he has not achieved his greatest popularity with his best work. The true reasons lie elsewhere. Germany, contrary to France and the English-speaking countries, escaped the Jansenist movement. Therefore, although neither Greene nor Mauriac nor Bernanos themselves may be Jansenistic, their preoccupation with the mystery of guilt goes back to the root and soil of their cultures. (There is probably, outside the world of Gogol and Dostoievsky, no more horrid presentation of the *mysterium iniquitatis* than *Brighton Rock.*) Let us not fool ourselves, evil has a universal fascination, disregarding all national frontiers and all borders of belief or disbelief. It is set off in a glare. We move "under the Sun of Satan."

Quite contrary to this, the world of storytellers like Ger-

trud von LeFort is, as we have said, a world of twilight.
The colours seem strangely subdued, the lines, at first sight,
look archaic. After you have stepped in you must give your
eyes time to adjust themselves. Then look around.

KARL STERN

PLUS ULTRA

PLUS ULTRA

BUT THEN, Reverend Mother, but then . . . I mean, every time His Majesty's eyes met mine, their steadfast gaze seemed to cause something to stir within me, or rather a tumult or storm to rise inside me, whether of delight or of horror I do not know—perhaps both together. No, I can swear, Reverend Mother, that I would not have known what to call it until that day when Her Highness the Lady Regent drew me into that conversation which you have ordered your obedient daughter to write down.

*

I saw the Lady Regent for the first time when Her Majesty's difficult pregnancy was nearing an end. She turned up unexpectedly in Valladolid to find the whole Court in a state of consternation, for the report had got about that the doctors had not much hope for Her Majesty, whose confinement had just begun.

She walked straight into the Empress's bedroom without even waiting to be announced. I saw her from behind as she rushed along. Her widow's veil had gone awry in her hurried journey and her glorious fair hair had burst out from under it. Then the veil slipped completely on to her neck leaving her luxurious head of hair quite free. It positively glowed in the gloomy passages of the castle, and as we followed the tall slender figure it was as though a candle were being carried along in front of us.

I did not see the Lady Regent's face until the following day when Her Majesty's confinement was already safely over—it had taken an unexpectedly favorable turn as soon as the Lady Regent had appeared. We—I mean Her Majesty's ladies in waiting—were presented to the Lady Regent afterwards. Her face was radiant, like the face of a young Empress Mother in whose arms the heir to the throne had just been laid. And actually all of us regarded her as the Empress Mother because His Majesty never called her anything but *"Ma très chère tante et mère."*

That day too her rebellious golden locks were breaking out from under her widow's veil. Everyone said that she looked just as radiant as she had looked when His Majesty had been elected Emperor. And all the world knew that that clever woman had played an important part in bringing about this triumph. She said a few gracious and pleasant words to each one of Her Majesty's ladies except me. To me she said not a word. She only looked at me, Reverend Mother, and though her eyes were not a bit like His Majesty's either in shape or color, their expression was so startlingly like his that my knees began to tremble and I thought I could never rise again after my deep curtsy.

4

That same evening the Mistress of the Robes sent for me. This lady was always saying I was much too young to serve at Court, but the Empress kept me all the same because I was an orphan from a great house. Several times I had heard the Mistress of the Robes say that it would be wise to send me back to the convent, so I was very frightened when she sent for me. You know, Reverend Mother, I was a quiet yet willful child, and even when I was here at school I had a great aversion to convent life, but after the life at Court, I felt an outright horror of it. The Mistress of the Robes looked at me coldly and severely; she did not say a word about the convent, but only told me that Her Majesty had released me from her service and transferred me to the service of the Lady Regent. That night I wept for many hours; I felt I would die if I had to go away from Valladolid.

I was not allowed to say goodbye to the Empress or to anyone else. Although I was not told this explicitly, I sensed it. No one seemed to take notice of the fact that I was dismissed; no one seemed to want to take notice of it. The Mistress of the Robes quietly beckoned me aside and instructed me to be ready to leave with Her Highness.

The Lady Regent's departure was not quiet and unexpected like her arrival. It took place with great ceremony and in the presence of the whole court. His Majesty himself accompanied his *très chère tante et mère* down the steps from the castle to her carriage. As instructed, I joined the ladies of her suite who were bowing gracefully and solemnly all around. I bowed too but no one took any notice

5

of me. It was as though I had become invisible; but at the same time I felt as if I were made of glass and everyone could see into my heart and know why I had been dismissed. Yet I myself did not know the reason, and I could not see into my own heart. By all that is holy I swear to you once again, Reverend Mother, that I could not! But I could see *with* my heart; I could look through myself with it just as if I were made of glass. For although I did not once dare to raise my eyes to His Majesty, I was suddenly aware that his eyes were fixed on me. The Lady Regent's carriage had now driven off and the rolling of its wheels could still be heard. His Majesty had turned back and now he walked slowly up the steps again to where I was waiting with another lady of Her Highness's suite for the second carriage to drive up.

I saw the slight youthful form, the pale noble face with the slightly open mouth which always looked a little thirsty, and the protruding underlip of his family. I saw . . . once more I saw this shattering look dart impulsively towards me out of his imperial loneliness, as it were, like a living fountain bursting through its stone basin. This glance enveloped my face, my body, my limbs, indeed my whole being, as the look of one human being can do to another but once in a lifetime. I wanted to return this look, yes, I wanted thus to embrace with my eyes His Majesty's face, form and whole being. I wanted to, did I say? It was as though everything within me was urging me to give that response at this last, this very last hour! For I had never given that answer before, Reverend Mother. The boundless delight mingled with horror which overcame me when His Majesty looked at me had prevented my doing so. Now too it stopped me. And yet I knew that the meaning of all the years of my life was concentrated into these few seconds.

But they were already past. The young Emperor, slowly walking up the steps, had reached the top as I descended with the other lady of Her Highness. I felt myself being lifted half unconscious into the carriage. And now the whole world became lost to me; all my glorious youth and all the hope of my future life. It was as though I were dead and were being thrust into outer darkness.

*

No one had said goodbye to me at the Court of Valladolid; now no one welcomed me at the Court of Malines. Apparently everyone had agreed to treat me as if I had always been there. The Lady Regent accepted my small services as if long used to them. Her ladies in waiting treated me with such friendly familiarity that they seemed to want to make me believe that Valladolid was only a dream. I fell in with the pretense myself seeing it was what they wished. Being a real little court lady I was able to do this, or rather I thought I could do it just as I could make my deep and solemn curtsy. For certainly anyone in attendance on an Empress has ample opportunity to practice the art of strict obedience! But how much silent rebellion can be hidden under the deepest curtsy, how wildly a heart can beat beneath the smooth satin of a court dress! Only at night when I slipped off this dress and lay down to rest did I drop my mask. I longed for this moment the whole day.

We, the Lady Regent's attendants, did not sleep in the Regency where she herself and her counselors had their bedchambers, but in the old palace of the Dukes of Burgundy right opposite it. Our rooms were close together along a corridor, just like convent cells. At first, this alarmed me somewhat, but the old ducal residence had stout walls and the sound of sobbing could not penetrate from one room to another.

The lane beneath my window lay in darkness, for in Malines the nights were not blue and crystal clear as in Valladolid, but pitch dark; there seemed no end to the darkness. The air which blew in the windows was damp and cold; often my feet were so icy cold that I could not sleep. I could hear hour after hour struck by the massive old tower clock of St. Rombold's. Often I fell asleep without saying my prayers; it was not that I wished to turn away from God but that all of a sudden there was no longer a place for God in my heart—it was too full of my yearning for Valladolid. When I got up in the morning my pillow was wet with tears; often I had wept the whole night through. These tears were a greater relief to me than sleep, but even in my sleep I wept. I used to get up in the early dawn to bathe my eyes so that people would not notice that I had been weeping all night. This took a long time because my tears kept on flowing and mingled with the cooling water.

The Lady Regent was a kind and considerate mistress to all her household, but she could not tolerate frivolous love affairs and flirtations, so her young ladies had to be very careful. On the other hand—so it was said—true deep love had her sympathy and she was ready to protect it. Well, neither of these things concerned me, I thought. Meanwhile the lady was a good mistress to me, too, but I was unable to feel any gratitude to her for this. Yes, Reverend Mother, I must confess that the only feeling for which there was room in my heart apart from my yearning for Valladolid was a deep grudge against the Lady Regent. For all the time I thought that it was at her wish that I had been dismissed from the service of the Empress, yet I could not imagine why she should desire me at her side. This malevolent feeling aften welled up so violently inside me that I was almost tempted to do her some harm.

She had a ruby glass goblet which her imperial nephew had presented to her after he had been elected Holy Roman Emperor. Now, in the evenings when I handed her this goblet containing the sleeping draught her physicians had prescribed for her restless nights, I felt overwhelmed with the temptation to let it fall, because I knew that she valued it very specially. Or I felt a longing to give her white Italian greyhound a little kick when I had to take him down to the garden and back again. I would have done so had the little dog not been able to protect himself—but he knew how to protect himself. His head was as fine and graceful as if carved from ivory, and his understanding too was very keen. He noticed everything and was allowed to be present even when the Lady Regent held council with the representatives of the estates of the realm. On these occasions he would lie at her feet as if asleep, but whenever one of the lords looked as though he would defy her, the dog would immediately start to growl. And every time my ill will against the Lady Regent surged up within me, the greyhound would immediately become aware of it! He would suddenly raise his slender head and look at me in a peculiarly watchful way—but without growling. And then my mistress too would raise her head and look at me. And every time this happened, Reverend Mother, all my ill will fled and died as in a shock of joy, for I felt as if His Majesty's eyes were looking at me. After that I asked myself again and again who it was that the Lady Regent loved so much. Who could it be? For only one whose love is deep—ineffably deep—can give another such a look. But in spite of the fact that I asked myself this—in spite of this—I still did not know what had happened to me, Reverend Mother. My confessor said later that I must have known it, but what does a monk understand about a girl's heart? By God, I had no knowledge of my own unless it be the knowledge that there are things of the heart which are unknowable.

*

When I slipped down the stairs of the old ducal palace in the morning to go over to the Regency, I had to pass by some apartments which I had been told His Majesty and his sisters, the young duchesses, used to occupy when the

Lady Regent was acting as mother to them. It was said that she still kept in these rooms the toys with which the royal children had played. I used to long to get into these rooms; indeed, my craving to do so was almost as great as my craving for Valladolid. I imagined that if I could see and touch the little toys just once my heart would grow lighter. So I always lingered there on my way to the other side and sometimes I imagined I heard a sound like the squall of a puppy when someone picks it up and presses it hard to his breast, or the striking of a note on the clavichord—you see, I knew that a clavichord had been procured for His Majesty when he lived there. And now it seemed to me that this old plaything had been stirred to life again. If so many courtiers had not been walking along the passages I would not have been able to resist the temptation to go in.

One day—it was the first time I had found the passage empty and quiet—I opened the door. I saw a little girl standing up in her bed holding a big doll in her arms. She seemed to me as strikingly familiar as the pictures of the little archduchesses, but at the same time frighteningly mysterious, as if a royal child were being kept hidden here. Yet the royal children had long since outgrown this nursery. I stood there so astonished, so confused that I could hardly keep calm.

"Who are you?" I blurted out.

"And who are you?" retorted the child in a haughty tone which seemed to mean: How dare you address me? Meanwhile a stout old nurse approached from the other side, and seeing my astonishment, said in a voice bursting with pride: "This is the little daughter of beautiful Joanna van der Gheenst. We have been ill for a long time, but tomorrow we're getting up for the first time. . . ."

Everything about the Malines Court was entirely without interest to me, yet I would have dearly loved to know who Joanna van der Gheenst was. I listened eagerly for mention of this name in the conversation of Her Highness's ladies in waiting, but it was never mentioned. People were just as silent about it as they had been about my arrival from Valladolid. And I was too proud to ask although I could not say why an enquiry about Joanna van der Gheenst should have hurt my pride, but actually it would have. As I said before, Reverend Mother, there is a certain knowledge which one can have unconsciously in one's heart.

*

The Lady Regent's maids in waiting did not spend as much time sitting at their embroidery frames as Her Majesty's ladies in Valladolid did. Our mistress needed us for other duties. Ambassadors from foreign courts and representatives of the estates of the realm, pompous clergy, defiant nobles and rich merchants, not to mention her own clever and prudent counselors, crowded her antechambers. For the Lady Regent ruled this country on behalf of His Majesty and all those who normally come to the ruler of the country came to her. So her ladies in waiting had to be always ready to receive those who came and entertain them with witty conversation or play the lute for them while they waited. Often, too, they had to put off unwelcome visitors tactfully or send them away. Hence, Her Highness's ladies held their little heads even higher than did the ladies of the Court of Valladolid, for they felt that they too knew something about the art of ruling. Moreover, they were wont to discuss many subjects which never troubled the heads of the Empress's ladies. I remember that it was from them that I first heard of the embarrassment which the terrible sack of Rome had caused His Majesty's government, and of the Holy Father's anger against that government; and that the Turks were threatening the frontiers of Hungary and that in spite of this there was no sign of a peace treaty with the King of France. For nowadays, so the ladies in waiting said, men were only able to make wars; they never managed to make peace. And as they said these things they put their little heads together as if they would erect a tent over the endangered world with their lace mantillas.

Every time a foreign courier arrived in the courtyard of the Regency my heart would beat as if it would burst, and I sought an excuse to stand by the window and peer out. For I always hoped he might be from the Emperor in Valladolid. Yes, Reverend Mother, I was so much of a child that I imagined that even the sight of the badge of an imperial courier should make me happy for a moment. Once when I actually saw this longed-for sign I rushed down the stairs into the courtyard, gathering up my train as I ran. Like an impetuous boy, I forced my way up so close to the prancing horse that the foam from its mouth blew into my hair, while Her Highness's greyhound, who had followed me, joyfully leapt and barked around me.

"Sir, give me the letter and I'll take it to Her Highness!" I cried. But he did not give it to me, and I had to go back upstairs in confusion.

The Countess Croy was standing at the top of the stairs and was about to scold me for holding up my train under my arm, but at that moment the Lady Regent came out of the door and said: "Countess dear, tell me who won the race, my greyhound or our little Arabella? I was watching from the window; do help me decide!" Of course the Countess Croy could not scold me then; her old grey face became as red as a young girl's, but I must have turned deathly pale for the Lady Regent looked at me again with that look—with that same look, Reverend Mother. Ah . . . I've already told you about it.

The Countess Croy was the first lady at the Court of the Lady Regent. She had served her mother when the latter was still the unmarried daughter of the Duke of Burgundy, and it was said that the Lady Regent had sat on her lap as a child. Hence she sometimes still addressed her as Grand Duchess, and the Lady Regent did not at all object to this, for the title reminded her that she was the daughter of an emperor. The Countess Croy loved the Lady Regent very dearly and for this reason she could not stand me. For though I myself always thought that I knew all about the rigorous art of silence and pretense—just as I knew how to make deep curtsies—she was perfectly well aware that I greatly disliked the Lady Regent and was always inwardly in rebellion against her. Actually, it was only in my own eyes that I was a thoroughly well-behaved little court lady. In reality I was a wild and desperate child whose thoughts and feelings were visible to everyone. And the Countess Croy had sharp eyes which saw behind every transgression against etiquette and every secret of the heart. Certainly she also knew about my nights of weeping—I could have sworn that she slept with her eyes open like an old hare. She constantly pointed out that the Lady Regent was far too indulgent with me, and that was certainly true. She did not speak to me very often, but she always stood up for me when the Countess Croy started to scold me. But like everything else, I resented this too for I always felt that she must surely know that she owed me some amends.

Yes, I was so resentful towards the Lady Regent that I could not admit any good in her. When others praised her —and she was greatly praised—I remained silent. I often heard it said that she ruled like a man, but I once heard a great lord saying: "No, she does not rule like a man. Her father, the Emperor Maximilian, tried to rule like a man and we resisted him. She rules like a woman, and that is how she has subdued us. For it is good for the refractory estates of this realm to be subject to a woman; with a man alone there is too much violence, but where a woman's hand restrains the man, a certain balance prevails." At this a third voice chimed in: "Yes, the secret of Her Highness is that she rules like a man and a woman in one. One would think she still had her husband beside her."

This pronouncement astonished me greatly because I had thought that the Lady Regent had forgotten her husband long ago. True, she always wore her widow's veil, but the rebellious golden locks kept peeping out as if to announce that the Lady Regent was not a real widow. Besides, she was always dressed in bright cheerfulness and she liked to see bright cheerful dresses around her. Even the walls of her study had to be hung with gay draperies. There were cheerful green trees woven into the tapestries, and on entering the room one almost expected to hear the birds singing. No, I could hardly believe that the Lady Regent was really a widow, and I thought I was pretty used to widows, for, since His Majesty had been fighting those terrible wars in Italy and France, there were many lonely women in Spain. And then there was Queen Joanna who had gone mad as she watched by the body of her dead husband. You yourself told me, Reverend Mother, that she had fled through the whole of Spain with her husband's coffin because she could not bear to see it laid in the tomb, and how she had the coffin opened again and again to kiss her own death on the mouth of her dead husband. When you told me about it, you said that Queen Joanna's action was terrible, but it pleased me, Reverend Mother, because I thought a true widow should love death. But the Lady Regent loved life. She loved the merry, industrious people whom she governed for His Majesty, she loved their wealth and their rebellious spirit, their headstrong nobles and their pompous merchants. She loved her own gay festive garments and the bright forest trees woven into the tapestries on her walls; she loved her clever little dog; she still loved the toys which had belonged to the royal children whom she had brought up. She loved them all, and especially her royal nephew. She loved his crown, and besides she loved—this was my latest discovery—that mysterious little girl whom I had met that time in the former apartments of the royal children.

The little girl was well again, for I saw her being taken for a walk in the gardens every day by her old nurse. Sometimes too she came over from the old ducal palace to the Regency. She would run gaily through the great rooms, bright with mirrors, to the Lady Regent's study, where the latter used to expect her at a certain time. If the Lady Regent was not ready, the mysterious little girl would knock at her door without any timidity. The ladies in waiting would put their fingers to their lips and whisper: "Hush! Her Highness is giving an audience!" But the old nurse who had followed the child would say impudently: "We don't take any orders here; for we're the daughter of beautiful Joanna van der Gheenst, and when we're grown up we also shall be a duchess."

The mysterious child had recognized me as the girl who had once penetrated into her room. Each time she saw me she would stand still as if rooted to the ground and look at me from head to foot with her big proud childish eyes, as if she were about to ask me once more: "And who are you?" But before I had time to speak she would suddenly wheel round like a top on her little pointed heels and run off at full speed. And to tell the truth I used to run in the

other direction, because we seemed nearly to frighten each
other to death.

The Lady Regent used to take the little one on her lap
and pet her tenderly. If I happened to be on duty at the
time and was standing beside her the thought would cross
my mind: that is just how the Lady Regent used to pet the
little grand-duchesses and that is just how she used to caress
her royal nephew's little head. Yes . . . just like that, and
with the same hands! And then I would suddenly feel a
longing to kiss the Lady Regent's hands quickly and un-
seen. Often this desire of mine was so violent that the
greyhound lying at her feet would notice it—and the Lady
Regent would notice it too. She would smile at me as if
she understood every thought which was going on inside
me, in fact as though she alone could understand me,
though I did not understand myself. And suddenly all my
piled up resentment towards her would collapse like a pack
of cards. I didn't know whether I loved her or hated her;
I only knew that she loved me.

*

Yes, the Lady Regent loved many people and many
kinds of people, and she loved them dearly, but I had come
to the definite conclusion that she did not love her late husband. Once, however, when I mentioned something to this
effect in a childishly reckless way to Madame von Bentink—
she was the one of Her Highness's ladies nearest to me in
age—she looked at me in astonishment and said: "But
have you never heard Brou mentioned, Arabella?"

Indeed I had often heard this name, for not only ambassadors from the courts and states came to the Lady Regent but also great artists from all over the world—architects, sculptors and painters, and these were the most welcome guests of all. She used to hold council with them for hours on end about a beautiful church which she was having built in her former duchy, distant Savoy. Her ladies said that this church was a matchless jewel; one would almost imagine that it was built, not of stone but of pure devotion and love; that it had blossomed forth like a mystical rose from the tender heart of a woman. And that, indeed, was so. "All the beautiful churches have been built by men," the ladies said, "but that one has been made by a woman. The builders have only carried out Her Highness's ideas. And that is why that church will never be finished, for the yearning from which it was born will never cease."

When the Countess Croy heard this talk her old grey face flushed again like that of a young girl. "That church will definitely be finished," she cried vehemently. "Are you godless girls blowing the same trumpet as the clerical dictators in Rome? As if the Lady Regent wasn't pious enough!"

But I had noticed long ago that the Lady Regent was not particularly pious, for I was always watching out for her faults, and although I was not at all pious myself, her lack of piety seemed to me to be a fault, and that made me glad. True, she fulfilled all the duties of her religion conscientiously. For after all, Reverend Mother, one can do that without being pious. Oh, indeed one can! It is so easy to go to church and kneel down and recite the proper prayers. But to raise one's heart to heaven when it is clinging to the earth by every fibre—that is hard. We went to Mass every morning in a dignified and devout procession, with the Lady Regent. She herself carried her father's prayer book in her hands, that famous volume illustrated by Dürer. Her ladies followed her, their heads, like hers, slightly bowed, their little trains gracefully arranged behind them, their rosaries daintily entwined in their fingers like pretty chains. And I was among them, looking as edifying as the rest, yet I was so far from God—immeasurably far—farther even than the distance from Valladolid to Malines.

Just as I had sensed that the Lady Regent was not really pious, I had also sensed that there was some mystery about the church at Brou. Once a French gentleman, the Ambassador of France in Malines, asked: "And what does His Majesty say to the building of the church?" Her Highness's ladies replied with evasive smiles, "No one knows, Monsieur." But the Countess Croy cut them short. "People know very well, dear children," she said. "His Majesty always agrees with his *très chère tante et mère.*" The French gentleman was obviously very pleased to hear this, but I don't believe he was thinking of the church in Brou at all; he was thinking that people were whispering that the Lady Regent should be entrusted with the making of the peace treaty between his King and our Emperor. For this conversation took place shortly before Her Highness set off for Cambrai.

Just at that time couriers were coming almost every day from Valladolid to Malines, but I no longer ran down to meet them in the courtyard. Instead I found an excuse to busy myself in the Lady Regent's study, even if it were only with brushing the smooth coat of her greyhound. At those times the Lady Regent never seemed to notice me although the Countess Croy made urgent signs to her to send me out of the room before she read out loud a letter to Her Highness. The Countess Croy often had to read the letters now, because Her Highness's beautiful warm eyes had been troubling her for some time and she had to use someone else's eyes when she wanted to read. At such times I had a hard struggle between my dislike of her and my longing to hear the letters, for I knew that my being allowed to remain depended on the Lady Regent. On the other hand, apart from a possible mention of His Majesty, I did not know what I expected to hear from the letters, because they all came from the dusty Chancellery.

Every time His Majesty's name was mentioned I received a violent shock as if a flash of lightning had struck beside me. Nevertheless I continued to listen with longing for his name. The Countess Croy was always rather excited when reading the letters from the royal Chancellery, for she lived in constant fear that they might announce the outbreak of a new war in spite of the fact that they were always about the making of peace and nothing else. But the Lady Regent too was sometimes agitated. The letters did not seem to please her at all, and though the Countess Croy had told the French gentleman that His Majesty was always in agreement with the Lady Regent, she did not seem to be in agreement with him at all now.

Once, when the Countess Croy was reading her correspondence aloud to her, one of her counselors was announced. The Countess immediately stood up and went out. I knew that I should do the same, because the counselors always wanted to see Her Highness alone. But I buried my face in the greyhound's coat and pretended not to see or hear anything. Her Highness made no comment on my presence; it was as though she knew what held me there. I should have thanked her for this in my heart and with my eyes, but it enraged me to be dependent on her kindness. And yet, I was dependent on it; she could have dismissed me from her presence as she had the Countess Croy. Why did she not do so? Did it mean that she sympathized with my yearning?

Meanwhile the Lady Regent's counselor had come in. "Just imagine, Sieur Des Barres," she cried as he approached her, "His Majesty still insists on the hard peace conditions of Madrid, he refuses to drop that clause about the Bourbons."

"As victor His Majesty actually has the right to humiliate France," replied Des Barres thoughtfully.

The Lady Regent pushed back her chair a little as she sometimes did when the stubborn representatives of the people tried to override her wishes. I say "tried," for she always got the better of them, and this, I must confess, was often quite wonderful.

"What do you mean by 'humiliating France'?" she asked. "The humiliation of France can scarcely be His Majesty's aim, can it? Ah, how sad it is to see the character of princes warped by victory!"

Des Barres bowed. "God bless Your Highness," he said. "God bless the kind and gentle heart of woman!"

But the Lady Regent cut him short. "No, Sieur Des Barres, you misunderstand me. It is not a question of the gentle heart of a woman here. It is a matter of recognizing that clemency and justice are only sound common sense. The Turks are approaching the frontiers of Hungary and threatening Christendom. It is not a matter of France alone, Sieur Des Barres, it is a matter of western civilization! His Majesty needs to have his hands free to turn back the Turks, but apparently His Majesty does not want to have his hands free."

At this Des Barres suddenly looked profoundly concerned. "Does that mean that Your Highness will not be going to Cambrai?" he asked.

The Lady Regent stood up. "On the contrary," she said, "it means that I must go to Cambrai." Then she added, with unusual warmth: "My God, when I think of the times I used to take His Majesty on my knee when he was a little boy. He was a self-willed, reserved child, but he was generous-hearted too, and even as a very small boy he had a sense of dignity! When I used to take his little head between my hands and teach him the words of greeting which later so delighted his grandfather the Emperor, he would repeat them word for word after me, even the words he did not like. I must take his head between my hands once more!"

*

There now came a period of great quietness in the old palace of the Dukes. The Lady Regent was away in Cambrai concluding a peace with the Old Queen Mother of France, each on behalf of the respective rulers—a peace which the sovereigns themselves had been unable to bring about. Meanwhile Her Highness's clever ladies in waiting had to be content to sit at their embroidery frames like the ladies in waiting in Valladolid.

The Lady Regent had left behind her a tapestry that was destined for the Knights of the Golden Fleece. The coat of arms of the ruling house was shown in the center with the devices of His Majesty and Her Highness to the right and left of it. The device of Her Highness was: *"Fortune, Infortune—fort une,"* but the device of His Majesty was *"Nondum."* The more facetious of Her Highness's ladies often made jests about this device. " '*Nondum*' means 'not yet'," they said, "and with such a device His Majesty could certainly never conclude a peace." I was annoyed by the derision of the lively-tongued ladies in waiting, for I knew from Spanish tourneys that His Majesty's device "*Nondum*" did not mean "There's time enough" but rather "Enough has not yet been achieved." It was not a word expressive of cautious tarrying, but rather the over-exuberant expression of too high an aim.

Once, when the ladies were enjoying their usual jibing, I jumped up like a little lion and told them that they did not understand the device. At this they giggled and nudged each other, but the Countess Croy rushed over to me and told me to keep silent and attend to my work; it was the device of Her Highness, which I had been ordered to embroider. But I was quite unable to understand this device, and consequently I made one mistake after another and had to undo my stitches again and again. This annoyed the Countess Croy very much, so she wrote out the motto and laid it beside me.

We had not yet finished the tapestry when the Lady Regent returned. She had really made peace, not the bad peace of Madrid, but her kind of peace—the famous *"Paix des Dames"* of Cambrai. So it seemed that the Countess Croy was right after all, and that His Majesty was in agreement with his *très chère tante et mère*.

The Lady Regent came along one day to look at our work. I heard her talking to the Countess Croy about His Majesty's device and I cocked my ears as if I were listening for the hoofbeats of the imperial couriers' horses. As I listened I bent deeper over my work, for now the Lady Regent was passing along from one lady to another, and I thought to myself: What shall I do if she passes me by? Suddenly I felt the greyhound's cold nose on my hand. The Lady Regent was standing beside me. She had already caught sight of the Countess Croy's little note.

"Well, Arabella, do you like my device so much that you've had it written out?" she asked.

"Your Highness, the Countess wrote it out for me because I was making so many mistakes in the stitches. But I don't understand the device," I replied defiantly.

"See if you will be more successful in understanding His Majesty's device," she said. "Now however it no longer reads *"Nondum"* but *"Plus ultra."* His Majesty changed it a few days ago because it was liable to be misunderstood, but I hear that you understood it."

Thereupon she instructed the Countess to have me work on His Majesty's device from then onwards. At this I felt I would like to throw my arms round the Lady Regent's neck, and yet I did not understand at all what she wished to convey to me by her words and her action. No, Reverend Mother, it was only a long time afterwards that I understood.

*

After the Lady Regent returned from Cambrai her ladies in waiting held their little heads even higher than before. "Yes, that was bound to happen!" they said. "Her Highness has helped a king and an emperor out of a deadlock at Cambrai. Now she will have to settle matters with the Holy Father too." For there was still no peace made between the Pope and the Emperor. Actually, a distinguished prelate from Rome was expected in Malines just then, to discuss with the Lady Regent the possibility of negotiations between His Holiness and His Majesty. The ladies were exultant; the Countess Croy alone seemed a little dejected as though the impending visit of the distinguished guest caused her apprehension.

It so happened that I was on duty in the Lady Regent's antechamber on the day when the prelate was having his audience. Before I entered the antechamber the Countess Croy told me to have the plans for the church in Brou ready at hand. Why, I did not know, for after all, the prelate was coming to discuss a peace treaty.

Well, when I was taking the portfolio from a locked cupboard I happened to let it fall. It opened, and the papers fluttered to the ground, and as I picked them up I saw the plans for the first time. First there was an absolutely plain drawing of the ground plan such as a master builder uses. Then there was a plan of the interior, likewise drawn in bare outline, as such plans are usually drawn. There were also sketches for the use of the stonemasons, showing all kinds of ornamentation and decoration, in fact, there were a great many of these. These sheets too were intended for the use of the craftsmen, not for the pleasure of the eye. Then came a page, beautifully tinted in soft yet definite colors. Surely this one was intended not for the hands of the sculptors, but for the eyes of others.

The colored drawing showed the completed church as seen from the inside. Looking at it, one could understand why the Lady Regent's ladies in waiting called this church a mystical rose. I should not have been surprised had I been told that it smelled of flowers as other churches smell of incense. And it really seemed as if it had been made by a woman's hand because it revealed so much tender love: every decoration and ornamentation, and every figure in it seemed to have been devised and formed by this love. It so filled the interior that at first I was quite unaware that there was anything vital lacking in the church. For in the choir, where the high altar normally stands, there stood a highly ornate tomb somewhat resembling a tabernacle. A stone figure of a sleeping man of great and noble beauty lay on top of the sarcophagus. He was surrounded by a crowd of little angels, who had taken his weapons from him so that he could lie more comfortably. He lay there quite defenseless as if in the arms of that great, gentle, yet strong love which enveloped him on every side. The great high church seemed only to exist for this slumbering man. Each decoration and ornamentation seemed to be focused on and devised for him as if some loving heart had again and again thought up new splendors to bestow on him. Suddenly I could only think—Oh, how the Lady Regent must have loved this man, and oh, how she must still love him! Who but she could love so much?

But now the Lady Regent called from the next room, and I went in to her with the portfolio for which she had asked. She was sitting in her high armchair behind which rose the splendid trees of the wall tapestry. As usual some of her fair hair was peeping from under her widow's veil, making her look as if little lights were dancing round her face and she was sitting in the midst of warm sunshine. The prelate did not look as if he was sitting in the sun; he looked more as if winter snow surrounded his still young head, and this gave his face a curious combination of grandeur and asceticism. I was handing my mistress what she required, but the prelate leaned forward and with a scarcely concealed air of authority, took the portfolio in his hand before she had time to do so. At the same moment the greyhound, who was lying at the Lady Regent's feet, jumped up growling. The Lady Regent flushed and suppressed an indulgent smile.

I made my curtsy and withdrew to the antechamber. There was an ominous silence in the room as I left it. For a while I could hear nothing but the rustling of the pages which the prelate was slowly turning over. You must know, Reverend Mother, that the anteroom was only divided from the audience chamber by a tapestry curtain, so that we could hear when we were called.

At last the cold voice of the prelate was heard. "Madame," he said, "just twelve months ago I had the honor of reminding Your Highness that His Lordship the Bishop was most anxious to consecrate the church at Brou and to consign it to its sacred use, but I still miss the high altar which Your Highness has presumably put on order long since."

The Lady Regent hesitated momentarily as if she were preparing a cautious evasion of the question. But at last she said candidly: "I have not given any order for the high altar, Monsignor."

The prelate too hesitated a few seconds before he replied, just as frankly: "Then Madame, the complaint we have received in Rome regarding Your Highness is justified. This church has been built, not to honor God but to honor your late beloved husband, as everyone says. Madame, this church is a pagan temple and I fear that the person who has built it is also pagan."

"And if I am a pagan, Monsignor," replied the Lady Regent with delicate irony, "and I do not say that I am—can the Rome of the Borgia pope and of a Leo X reproach me?"

Now the cold voice of the prelate betrayed an undertone of restrained passion. "Your Highness is mistaken," he said. "We are no longer the luxurious Rome of the Borgia pope and of Leo X. The Emperor's hordes of mercenary soldiers have exacted a terrible atonement from us. With the *Sacco di Roma* a new generation has come into being, and this generation has suffered unprecedented chastisement. Truly, in the body of the Eternal City there is no member which has not done penance—we priests have turned grey-haired in the course of that chastisement. But His Imperial Majesty will have to do penance too. One cannot sin against what is holy and go unpunished."

The Lady Regent's chair could be heard being pushed back as it was wont to be before the defiant representatives of the people. "No one can regret more than His Majesty does," said the Lady Regent quickly, "that his victory should have led to the sacking of the Eternal City. His Majesty did not want that."

Now I seemed to perceive from the prelate's voice that a triumphant smile crossed his face. "Your Highness speaks of an imperial victory," he said. "I regret to have to point out for the second time that you are mistaken. His Imperial Majesty was not the victor in Rome as he had been in Pavia; on the contrary, he was vanquished by his own army—for by the *Sacco di Roma* His Majesty forfeited his victory. A beaten and imprisoned king of France is a beaten and imprisoned king, but a defeated and imprisoned pope becomes forthwith a glorious and powerful pope. All Christianity will throw itself at the feet of such a pope as if Christ Himself had been insulted in him." Then he added with emphasis: "His Holiness has sent to Valladolid his conditions for giving Absolution to His Majesty. That does not concern us here. Therefore let us return to the question of the church at Brou."

"Are you speaking to me on behalf of the Holy See?" the Lady Regent interrupted him.

"Not yet," replied the prelate significantly, "but it may be that I shall soon have to speak to Your Highness on behalf of the Holy See. As yet I am speaking to you as a friend and a counselor who has come to warn you."

I did not hear what followed immediately. Finally I caught the words: "Madame, I recommend that you offer to God the grief of your widowhood, renounce your desire for earthly love, and turn your mind to the welfare of your soul. For a true widow should die to the world."

Again there was the sound of the Lady Regent's chair being pushed back, and immediately afterwards I heard her light good-humored laugh. "Yes," she said in a jocular tone, "I know you priests! You have hardly thrown off the bare-faced sensuality of the Borgia period when you start talking once more of contempt of the world. In your eyes everything exists only to be overcome and sacrificed to heaven. But a person who is to help shape and govern the world dare not despise it but must on the contrary be able to love the world and embrace it."

"Very well," said the prelate calmly, "let us leave aside the question of denying the world. But how about the question of God? Your Highness is building to honor a mortal something which is due only to the Eternal. You are shrinking from erecting an altar to your Creator; you are rejecting God. That is the frightful secret of Brou which Rome will not tolerate."

Again silence fell between them; then the Lady Regent said quietly yet proudly: "I do not reject God, Monsignor. How could a human being do such a thing? But there is no place in my heart for God. Perhaps this heart of mine is too narrow. Perhaps it may be enlarged by grace one day, but as yet it is unable to embrace more than my beloved husband. Because he was a man, I love mankind; because he was a ruler, I wish to be a ruler; and because for me he is not dead, I can live. For me the church of Brou is no tomb; it is the place where death has been vanquished, because for those who truly love there is no separation, Monsignor. Love eliminates all separation. In Brou I can still tend the resting place of my husband. There I can lavish my love on him; there I can offer him again and again everything which he loved in me, obtain for myself the will and the strength to live. For I say once more that one whose task it is to form and govern a state in this world must also be able to embrace the world. And I embrace it in my beloved husband."

There was something compelling and fascinating in her declaration, something in its sheer excess which made me shudder, a devotion and gentle strength which carried me away. It reminded me of Queen Joanna throwing herself on her husband's coffin. But the Lady Regent did not want to kiss death as Queen Joanna did—only life. I certainly felt and realized the horrifying aspect of her words, but I was not repelled by them. On the contrary, they made my heart rejoice.

I could still hear the frigid voice of the prelate, but only as if from very far away. "Madame," he said, "I thank you for the frankness of your confession. I think I understand you perfectly now. Your highness should abandon your state of widowhood and enter the state of matrimony once more. Your Highness misses the joys of marriage, and unfortunately you have not known as yet the blessing of children. If Your Highness could decide to choose another husband the matter of Brou would right itself."

At this the Lady Regent sprang to her feet, quickly, youthfully, almost stormily; I could hear the rustle of her brocade dress. "Monsignor," she cried excitedly, "I regret every word I have said to you! Love does not mean either the choice of a state of life or sensual pleasure. Neither does one love for the sake of having children. Love is a ray of light which breaks in upon us from another world to

33

light up ours, and I will trust to this ray during my earthly journey. God will not condemn me because of my love. And now we shall end this conversation."

The prelate left the room immediately.

I was still so stunned and intoxicated by what I had heard that it did not occur to me to kneel down for his blessing, which he gave me casually as he passed through. How can I explain my state to you, Reverend Mother? The words of the Lady Regent were seething exultantly within me. Now I was no longer saying to myself: "Oh, who could love as she does?" For *I* could, yes, I could! It was as though all the doors of my inner being flew open like the gilded doors of a shrine, and I looked down into my own heart for the first time. Involuntarily I spread out my arms —I felt as though I were embracing the beloved image within them. Oh, Reverend Mother, I was so happy! I realized at last what had happened to me. I knew at last that I loved, and I knew whom I loved!

Suddenly I heard the warm soft voice of the Lady Regent beside me asking: "Arabella, did you hear my conversation with the Monsignor?"

I trembled so violently that I had to hold on to the top of the table in front of me; but it too shook when I touched it, making the bowl which stood on it tinkle. "Oh, Madame!" I gasped. "You know, Madame, I dared not leave my place here."

"Yes, I know, Arabella," she replied. And she took my head between her two hands, bent it a little back and said: "I know, I know everything." Oh, that look . . . that look,

Reverend Mother! Now at last I understood its secret! Only a person who has fallen hopelessly in love can look at one like that—and the Emperor had looked at me like that! Not only did I love: I was loved! Once more an incomparable feeling of joy came over me. It was almost like a faintness robbing me of all my strength, of all my ability to understand the monstrousness of this love. I could only comprehend the love itself. Everything else seemed as if destroyed, trampled on and vanquished. I felt I would die. The bowl on the table to which I was holding, shook as if it would break, and if the Lady Regent had not put her arm around me I would have sunk to the ground.

She held me silently for a short while. Then she said: "I brought you here like a little sleeping child, Arabella, and you were angry with me for that because you did not understand either yourself or me. But now you have awakened; now, I can talk to you. They were going to put you into a convent, but that would have been fatal for you because there you would have had to die to your love. But I loved your love; I wanted it to live, and it can live, because for love there is no separation. You have just heard that. You dare not demand anything, but you may love, and that is enough. Do you understand now why I brought you here with me?"

But I did not understand her. No, Reverend Mother, I did not understand her at all now! How could she compare me to herself? She had a husband whose love she had enjoyed, and he was buried in the tomb, whereas I was to bury in my heart someone whom I had never embraced!

She had tasted every happiness and every joy. I had only the bliss of yearning. She could still show tenderness towards the dead, but I . . . I could never, not even once, return the look of love of the living. I began to weep as if my heart would break.

She pressed me to her like a mother. "Poor child! Poor child!" she said. "Can I do nothing for you but commend you to the strength of your own love?"

I took myself from her arms. I was beside myself. "Madame, how can you ask such a thing? Surely you know what you can do for me?" I cried. "Oh, send me back to Valladolid, send me back! Grant me just one day there— one single day! I beg of you on my knees!" While I was speaking I felt as if my own heart were enveloping me in flames and that I would burn up if I could not get away. "Send me back! Send me back!"

She looked at me sadly, and at last she said: "It wouldn't help you, Arabella, if I were to do as you ask. For who do you think it was that wanted to put you into a convent?"

Without hesitation I replied: "It was Her Majesty the Empress."

"No, it was the Emperor," she replied.

What was I to understand from this? For after all, I was loved.

She guessed my thoughts. "It was precisely because you were loved," she said.

Was it for my sake? Was it in order to spare me? Or was it to protect me? These questions shot through my mind. Ah, Reverend Mother, a girl in love always thinks that the beloved can act only out of love for her!

Now the Lady Regent shook her proud head angrily. "No, my foolish child," she said, "it was not for your sake. It was for the sake of the Empire." Her words fell like the shadow of an austere unfamiliar sanctuary between herself and me. "Do you know what the Empire means?" she asked. I did not dare to reply. After that nothing more was said.

*

From that day on, Reverend Mother, I thought only of how I could flee to Valladolid. Tears no longer mingled with my nightly dreams. In my dreams I now swung myself onto a swift little Arab horse and rode in the darkness through the country. It was the same nimble little horse which I used to ride at the royal hunts. For you know, Reverend Mother, I was an ardent horsewoman; at the Court they used to say I rode like a boy. My swift little horse came bounding into my bedroom every night as if by magic and with its hooves beat against my bed. It still had on the same richly ornamented saddle which had once charmed my childish heart, and I was soon on its back galloping through the damp misty Flanders night mile after mile along the road by which I had once come here in the Lady Regent's carriage.

But then, as I trotted up the road from Salamanca to Valladolid in the grey dawn of the morning and saw the high walls of the Simanca Castle rise up before me, suddenly everything around me would grow pale and wan. And when I would arrive at the gate of the castle, someone whom I no longer recognized would be standing there and would ask me: "Do you know what the Empire means?" And I would have to turn back in silence, for I did not know.

But when I woke up I did not know why I had turned back—nor did I want to know. The whole day long I would ponder how I could make my dream come true. It is probably like that with the birds, Reverend Mother, when they get the great urge to migrate over the sea, or with the plants when the sap stirs within them in spring and the tender sprout pushes its way through the crust of earth. And so it was that they found me one morning in the early dawn lying under a green tree some miles from Malines, and brought me back to the Lady Regent's court. First the Countess Croy questioned me as to how I came to be lying under that green tree. I could not explain it, even to myself; I could only say that the little Arab horse of my dreams had thrown me off there. At this the Countess said, "We shall have to lock you up at night, Arabella, if you take your dreams so seriously that you run after them into the dark night."

Then the Lady Regent sent for me. Before I went to her the Countess Croy said to me: "Pull yourself together, Arabella. Her Highness has had many worries recently, and you must not add to them by your willfulness." I did not take her words to heart at all, because I had been seething with anger against the Lady Regent again for not having listened to my plea to send me back to Valladolid.

When I entered her room she had the mysterious little girl on her lap again. The old nurse was standing proudly by, her face beaming with joy as if her darling were sitting on the throne which was her due. When the Lady Regent noticed me she put the child down, kissed her and told the nurse to take her away. The child followed the old woman reluctantly. As she passed me by she looked at me defiantly as if to say: "How dare you supplant me here?" But it seemed to me that now, for the first time, I could give a definite name to the sensation of fear which the sight of the child caused me.

Now the Lady Regent was speaking. I had expected that she would reprimand me for my flight, as the Countess Croy had done. But she only said lightly and almost jocosely: "I hear, Arabella, that you made off at night on a little Arab horse and were found in the morning under a green tree. And I also know the direction your road took. So you do not yet realize what the Empire means?"

While she was saying this to me, the voice of the mysterious little girl could be heard outside the door, mingled with that of her nurse who tried in vain to reason with her. Then the little girl pushed open the door and was about to rush up to the Lady Regent again. But the latter looked at her sternly and said: "For shame, *ma petite!* Have you forgotten who you are?" At this the little girl turned pale and withdrew ashamed and struggling with her tears. But I heard the nurse whispering to her in the

39

doorway: "Hush, love, you are still the daughter of the beautiful Joanna van der Gheenst!"

When the child had gone out, the Lady Regent continued as though nothing had happened. "The Empire, Arabella, is the power to which the Emperor himself in the first place must submit. As sovereign he dare not permit the slightest stain to besmirch his name. Do you understand at last what I mean?"

I remained silent, choked with fear and jealousy. Suddenly I heard my voice asking: "And who is Joanna van der Gheenst?" It sounded as though someone had dragged the question by force from my lips. At once I knew that I had asked for my own death sentence. Already the Lady Regent was pronouncing it.

"Joanna van der Gheenst," she said calmly, "is the mother of the little girl who was with me just now. The child was born an Emperor's daughter before there was an Empress at the Court. Since there has been an Empress at the Court there can no longer be a Joanna van der Gheenst there. Do you understand now that the Emperor is the very first person who has to submit to the Empire?" She said these words very seriously, in an almost distant tone, but then her voice became kind again. "Console yourself, my child," she added. "You are not suffering alone, you see."

But I was not consoled, Reverend Mother, I was not consoled at all. For I was indeed a deluded person, and no one can help the deluded but everything encourages the delusion. I had asked for and received the death sentence on my love. But I did not die because of this—love cannot die. Again and again it finds a way of escaping death. Of all that the Lady Regent said to me only one thing had really penetrated my mind, and that was that there was no longer any Joanna van der Gheenst in Valladolid. And that was enough to relieve me. Yes, Reverend Mother, I was bewitched, indeed almost obsessed. If I had not actually been locked up by the Countess Croy every night at that time, I would not have needed my dream-horse to help me to flee a second time.

But there were other reasons too which prevented my doing so, for a few days later the Countess Croy informed me that I was to hold myself in readiness to accompany the Lady Regent on a journey. "Her Highness is of the opinion that you need some special diversion," she said with visible reluctance. "Do you understand the very special favor which is being shown you?" The Countess Croy did not say where the journey would be taking us, and I should have preferred to cut out my tongue rather than ask her. In any case it was a matter of complete indifference to me—I was not interested in any place which was not Valladolid.

*

In the following days the Lady Regent very hurriedly discharged some government matters, and put others aside until later on, among these the answering of various letters from the Imperial Chancellery which had recently been piling up. Meanwhile all kinds of reports were circulating regarding the impending journey but no one really knew the destination except her counselors and the Countess

Croy. Of course Her Highness's ladies did not like to admit that they did not know; they still held their little heads with their lace mantillas just as high as before and put on very important airs.

"His Majesty is in need of Her Highness's help," I heard them whispering.

This remark made me take notice at last. "Is Her Highness going to Valladolid, then?" I burst out in spite of myself.

The ladies smiled meaningfully. "Yes, where else would Her Highness be going?" they said. "We're not supposed to talk about it but we just know it."

Now I was utterly happy—so happy that my happiness almost hurt me. You will be hardly surprised at this, Reverend Mother, for you already know that I was as one bewitched! Now I did not mind in the least when the Countess Croy locked me into my room at night; I sang and laughed in my prison and sometimes a cry of joy actually escaped me on the stairs, for I thought I noticed that the Countess Croy was suddenly less attentive in matters of etiquette about which she was normally so severe and watchful. But a short time before they used to say that she had laid down rules as to when Her Highness's little dog might bark and when it might not, and that he should be instructed to walk backwards out of the door in the presence of princely personages. But now she overlooked every *faux pas* at Court. She seemed to have become shortsighted where etiquette was concerned, but farsighted in her solicitude for Her Highness, as if some secret misfortune were threatening the latter from somewhere far away.

"If only Her Highness had not dismissed the Roman prelate so hastily that time," I heard her complain to Des Barres. "Ah, I'm afraid, I'm so afraid! My only consolation is that Her Highness can rely on His Majesty as if he were her own son."

Again I listened intently at mention of His Majesty.

"Yes, Her Highness can always depend on His Majesty behaving as a son," replied the Counselor, Des Barres, "but this son is also an emperor and as such is *Defensor Ecclesiae*."

His reply seemed to alarm the poor Countess. "But His Majesty himself is not yet reconciled with His Holiness," she objected. She seemed to be trying to flee from the thought which Des Barres had expressed.

"That is true," replied the latter, "but His Majesty will become reconciled. It is a matter which concerns the unity of Christendom. The heresy in Germany makes a General Council of the Church necessary, and His Majesty will make every sacrifice to facilitate this, and he will require others to do the same." Then he added significantly: "The Lady Regent wished to bring up an Emperor—and she has brought up an Emperor."

After this conversation the Countess Croy became even more uneasy and more absent-minded than she had been, indeed she became so absent-minded that one morning she quite forgot to unlock my door which she had been locking every night since my attempted flight. I was glad to have this quiet day and I spent it so happily daydreaming about my journey to Valladolid, that I felt neither hungry nor thirsty. And I kept so quiet that no one noticed my imprisonment. Only late in the evening the Countess remembered her omission; by that time the whole court had become convinced that I had run away again. Meanwhile the Lady Regent had given orders that I should be brought to her as soon as I was found.

She was already in her nightdress, and was sitting barefooted in front of her mirror. Her maid had just finished combing her hair and it hung over her back and shoulders like a heavy golden cloak. It was the first time that I had seen her without her widow's veil. I had not spoken to her since our fateful conversation and now she seemed changed somehow, as though in taking off her regal robes she had also cast off her character as Princess and Regent. She looked almost like a young girl. Indeed she really looked like a bride. There was something hopeful, something joyfully anxious yet courageous and rapturous about her. Yes, Reverend Mother, that is just how she must have looked on her wedding day.

But I too was as full of joyful suspense as a bride, for I would soon be traveling to Valladolid with Her Highness. She noticed my buoyant spirits and said: "My poor little prisoner, in the future my good Croy shall not have to lock you up. I shall watch over you myself. For you know, don't you, that you are to accompany me on my journey? Are you pleased with me at last?"

I kissed her hand, for God knows I was pleased. Even the greyhound noticed my happy emotion. He jumped up wildly; one would imagine that the courtly little animal knew already that the Countess Croy would no longer be supervising his etiquette.

While I was laughingly warding off the dog, the sound of horses' hooves became audible in the courtyard below. The Lady Regent listened, visibly startled. A few minutes later a letter was brought in to her. I recognized the Imperial seal, and actually, it was the seal of His Majesty himself, not the seal of the Chancellery. This startled the Lady Regent even more. She immediately broke the seal, but because of her bad sight she could not read the letter.

"Quick, quick, read it to me!" she urged, passing it to me. I felt her hand trembling as she did so; my own were trembling too. Now I was actually holding in my hand one of those letters which I had once tried unsuccessfully to wrest from the courier. I saw that restrained, aristocratic, yet quite legible handwriting of His Majesty. I saw that famous proud signature—*I, the Emperor.* For a moment my eyes too seemed to fail. I marveled that my voice did not break as I read:

Madame, *très chère tante et mère!*

It was the gentle but deep wisdom of woman which convinced me in those days at Cambrai that the self-restraint of the victor represents his real and finally decisive victory. I do not say the mercy and generosity of the victor, for the sober experiences of the ruler make these words hard to tolerate. It was simply a matter of worldly common sense. The same wisdom which demanded at Cambrai a propitiatory peace with

France because of the threat from the Turks, now demands for the sake of Christian unity an effort at reconciliation with regard to the *Sacco di Roma*. I have complied with the severe demands of His Holiness regarding the reinstatement of the Medici in Florence as well as the no less difficult conditions of the Holy See regarding Parma, Piacenza and Milan.

There still remains the small but explicitly stated wish of the Holy Father regarding the church at Brou. I have also agreed to the fulfillment of this wish. I therefore find it my duty to request Your Highness to kindly desist from your intended journey there, and to refrain from entering Brou until the wish of His Holiness regarding the church there has been fulfilled. I recommend Your Highness to take the necessary steps to comply with that wish at once. I know well that I cause you great pain by this communication. To give you a command runs counter to my feelings of childlike devotion, but I cannot conceal the fact that I shall have to command you if you cannot bring yourself to command yourself. Permit me, then, to close with those weighty and compelling words which, when striving to persuade me on the question of the Peace of Cambrai, you suggested I should adopt as my device: *Plus ultra*.

I, the Emperor

When I finished reading the Lady Regent sat there as if benumbed. Suddenly she jumped up, snatched the letter from me and crumpled it in her hand.

"Call the Countess," she ordered breathlessly. "We're setting out for Brou early in the morning."

"For Brou, Your Highness?" I stammered. "For Brou? But we were going to Valladolid!"

"No, we were going to Brou," she replied angrily. "I want to visit my husband! Call the Countess!"

Numbed with bitter pain, I stood motionless, unable to carry out her order.

In spite of her agitation, she gradually realized my disappointment. "Foolish child!" she said half angrily, half compassionately. "So you still refuse to understand what the Empire means? You still refuse to bow to it!"

She stopped short and looked at me with an almost horrified expression: from the frightful depths of my disappointment there had risen straight as a candle, a vivid flame of triumph. For she too was refusing to understand what the Empire meant; she too would not submit to it. I could have hurled this charge in her face, but she had already read my thoughts. In a completely calm and immensely majestic tone she said: "Very well, Arabella, pass me my sleeping draught and then go and call the Countess."

She sounded as if nothing at all had happened. I was overwhelmed with a desire to humble her, to bend that proud head under the same yoke beneath which she wanted to force mine. With trembling hand I took the ruby goblet, that precious gift from the Emperor which her maid had already filled.

And now everything passed out of my control. I did not decide on what was to happen; it just happened. I raised the Imperial goblet. I raised it high in the air as if I were drinking a toast to her. *"Plus ultra!"* I cried in a resounding voice. I scarcely had time to notice how deathly pale she had become when I felt her snatch the cup from my hand. The next instant it crashed to the ground.

I think that she made a sign for me to leave. I still remember going towards the door in silence, but even before I reached it, I heard a faint cry. Turning round, I saw that the Lady Regent's face was distorted by sharp physical pain. Blood was trickling to the ground. She had cut her bare foot with a fragment of the broken goblet.

*

And now, Reverend Mother, you already know what all the world knows—I mean the Lady Regent's terrible end, caused by that apparently very slight and, what seemed to those surrounding her, fortuitous wound. The following day she was unable to get up, nor the next day either. On the third day a violent fever set in, and the doctors were helpless to stay its disastrous course. Soon it was no longer a secret that gangrene had developed in the injured limb and was threatening to poison her whole body.

Permit me to refrain from describing my own state. I had alternately loved and hated the Lady Regent; now I knew that even my hate was really love. I wept my eyes out at the thought of her pain—for of course it was my cry which had aroused her anger. The desire which had animated me to speak those words had been fulfilled: she had realized that she too had not wanted to bow to the Empire—but she had to pay for this with her life! I was consumed by a profound but helpless remorse. Yes, for the first time I had to face remorse—and I did not know how to face it! For days it replaced every other feeling within me, even the desire to return to Valladolid. I would often furtively walk behind the Countess Croy as she hurried into the sick room with bandages and medicines. My one wish was to be allowed to follow her in that I might beg Her

Highness to forgive me. But the Countess did not notice me; no one gave me a thought. All were occupied with their own anguish or their anxiety for the invalid. Only the small proud daughter of the beautiful Joanna van der Gheenst, who now was as forsaken as I, sometimes threw her arms round my neck when we met in the deserted halls and chambers of the Regency, and we would weep together like two children who had always been good friends.

On the seventh day I heard a scratching at my door. When I opened it Her Highness's little greyhound was standing outside looking up at me with his sad eyes. I knelt beside him and wept into his velvety coat. He freed himself from me in a graceful and grave manner and with almost an air of reproach, and then silently went back the way he had come, turning around and looking back at me again and again as if demanding that I should follow him. I did so, and he led me down the stairs and over into the Regency. There he stopped outside Her Highness's bedroom, and scratched at the door. I opened it for him. He slipped in and went up to Her Highness's bed, the curtains of which were completely drawn back.

But I could not see the Lady Regent because her counselors were standing around her bed. Her notary was present too, and I could hear her dictating a letter to him. When I appeared two waiting women stood up from their places near the foot of the bed and were about to send me out, but the Lady Regent stopped dictating and said in a weak but very clear voice: "I have been expecting Arabella. I wish her to remain." Then she continued dictating: "The

hour has come, Sire, when I am preparing to accept the
final call from God. My conscience is at peace and my only
pain is being unable to look upon Your Majesty once more
in this life. I leave to Your Majesty, as my sole heir, the
country which has been entrusted to me, and which I now
surrender to you not only intact but augmented in honor
and riches, after a regency for which I hope to obtain a
reward from God and thanks from Your Majesty. Once
more I commend peace to Your Majesty, especially peace
with the King of France. I commend to Your Majesty all
my faithful servants, men and women, and finally I commend to you the dear church at Brou as the resting place of
my beloved husband, at whose side I myself wish to be
laid to rest. I therefore beg of Your Majesty, as a last
favor. . . ."

She was going to add something, but her strength suddenly failed her. She remained completely silent for a few
minutes, while those of her waiting women who were present tried to revive her with some strong smelling restora-
tive. Then, when she had come to herself somewhat,
though still very weak she continued in a low voice:
". . . With this earnest petition I beg to take leave of Your
Majesty in this world."

The document was handed to the Lady Regent for her
to sign, then her counselors, deeply moved, kissed her hand
reverently and left the room. Now I could see the bed. The
Lady Regent was lying exausted with her eyes closed; her
face almost submerged in the great mass of loosened hair.
With her hands folded she looked as she would look later

on her tombstone. The greyhound had nestled down at her feet and looked as if he wished to die with his mistress. And actually, the faithful little animal only survived her by a few days. Some moments passed, then the Lady Regent opened her eyes once more and said in a clear but even weaker voice: "Now I wish to bid farewell to my ladies in waiting one by one. I will begin with the youngest."

And now, Reverend Mother, all those in the room went out, and it seemed to me wonderful that they did so and I was allowed to be alone with the dying lady. But probably no one had the courage to oppose her last orders. I knelt down by her bedside. "Oh, Madame," I sobbed, "Oh, Madame, I have killed you! If I had remained silent as I passed you the cup, you would now be able to travel to Brou to your husband."

She whispered: "No, not you . . . the Emperor handed me that cup. He had to do so; his high rank demanded this of him. I am dying because I did not drink of the cup willingly, but I am dying willingly. No, do not reproach yourself, my child. You have only helped me to push open a door. For now I may journey to Brou. Even the Emperor will raise no objection any more. I shall be united with my husband, never to part from him again."

While she was speaking her countenance became more and more transfigured. An expression so joyful that it seemed to me not of this world at all, broke through the shades of death which lay upon her. Again she seemed to my eyes like a bride on her wedding day, or perhaps like a saint on the day of her death. All of a sudden I no longer knew: Was she speaking of the memorial chapel in Brou or of the happiness of heaven; of rest in the grave by the side of her husband or rest with God? Suddenly I remembered her last words to the Monsignor.

She looked at me with a curiously initiated smile. You know, Reverend Mother, they *do* say the dying have second sight! "Yes, my wild little Arabella," she gasped, "yes, indeed, I have not been deceived in my confidence in love. Now, as I lie dying, God has opened my heart. If I were able, I would now build the altar to Him, but the Emperor will do that for me. I have asked him as a last favor to do so. And now it only remains for me to open the door for you. For you must know, my child, there is in all eternity only one love, and that comes from heaven. Even if this world calls it earthly love, God accepts it as if it were offered to Himself." At these words her voice faded like that of someone moving away, and her face took on a different hue. It was as though the joy of heaven were already veiling her features. No one ever died a more holy death than the Lady Regent, Reverend Mother! Once more she whispered: "Yes, I love God . . . I love Him . . . I have always loved Him . . . I have loved Him in His image. . . ." And then she sank into deep unconsciousness. And you know, Reverend Mother, that she never regained consciousness after that.

I shall pass over the long, sorrowful ceremonies which followed the Lady Regent's death, and the first preparations for the dispersion of her former royal household. Most of Her Highness's ladies decided to return to their families, others were being taken over into the Court of the Empress, and others again were kept on for the future Court of the Archduchess Marie, the widowed Queen of Hungary, whom it was said His Majesty intended to appoint as regent in succession to Her Highness. The little daughter of beautiful Joanna van der Gheenst also left the old ducal court and was given into the hands of a Spanish noblewoman to be brought up.

My future alone seemed to be untouched by all the changes. I had no family to whom I could return and there was never any question of my being taken over by the Empress or recommended to the Archduchess Marie. With the Lady Regent no longer there, I seemed, in a sense, an embarrassment to everyone. True, the Countess Croy now took a very motherly interest in me, not for my own sake, however, but because of her great and undying love for the Lady Regent who she knew had been so fond of me. And certainly it cannot have been easy for the Countess to be so nice to me, because she had never cared for me very much. Besides, she could not forgive me for having been privileged to hear Her Highness's last words, more especially as I had jealously kept these words from her and from everyone else, for after all they touched my own fate too closely.

But in the end the Countess Croy suggested a plan for my future: she said that it would be best for me to enter a convent. Of course I struggled against this proposal like a little animal whom someone tries to drown. She grew silent and sighed, but returned to the subject again and again. Indeed she kept on urging me with painful persistence. Soon I was to know why. For about the time that the Countess began recommending the convent to me the news went round the Court that the Emperor was coming to Malines to settle personally some affairs of the realm which had been left in abeyance owing to the Lady Regent's death. This had to be done before Queen Marie could take over the Regency.

You will probably think, Reverend Mother, that the death of the Lady Regent and the painful remorse I suffered would have changed me. Ah, no, nothing in me had changed. The black mourning crepe and the remorse had smothered my passion for a short time. Now it broke over me with double force: The Emperor was coming to Malines, so I would not have to flee to Valladolid— Valladolid would be in Malines. At last my eyes would meet the longed-for loving glance, at last I would return this loving glance for the first time. Now the Countess Croy did not mention the convent any more. My radiant face, which must have looked rather odd and noticeable under my mourning veil, probably discouraged her from doing so. Ah, poor Countess Croy! How desperate she must have felt over me! She did not let it be seen, however; but just those days she often asked me to accompany her to the Convent of the Annunciation. For the mortal remains of the Lady Regent were being kept in the chapel there until the memorial church in Brou would be ready to receive them. We would kneel down together and pray beside the silent coffin, and lay flowers upon it. Then we would return to the Regency.

One day, when we had finished our usual prayers, the Countess whispered to me that I must stay a while longer with my dead mistress as she had to go and see the Prioress. I did as I was told, and she went away. But she did not return. Instead, a gentle young nun came, took me by the hand in a friendly way, and conducted me, not as I expected, to the waiting Countess, but to the Prioress. The latter informed me in the same gentle and friendly manner that I was to be the dear guest of herself and the sisters for a little while, but she was sure time would not hang too heavily on my hands as they would do everything to make my stay pleasant.

Of course I understood at once that I was a prisoner: it was only a few days before His Majesty was due to arrive. I was a prisoner, treated with kindness and gentleness, but ruthlessly immured. The barred windows and the knowledge that the gate of the Enclosure was well locked, left no doubt that they desired to put me away while His Majesty was in Malines. Of all the disappointments which I had met with up till then, this was the most cruel, the most torturing. Every night I tugged in vain at the iron bars of my window until my hands became helpless with pain and my eyes closed with exhaustion. Even my little dream horse did not succeed in breaking through these pious walls. Only a miracle could open my prison. In the meantime the Emperor was entering Malines.

But now the miracle happened! A few days later the Countess Croy stood before me in the convent guest room. Well, Reverend Mother, I had been clever and proud enough not to let my pious jailers notice my indignation over my compulsory stay with them. For in the first place, those good women, who knew nothing of the world, very probably could not have refused to be burdened with me, and besides, I knew from the outset that tears would only have made them watch me with more vigilance. I silently submitted to all the rules of their convent—I imagine the good sisters believed I felt quite contented with them.

It was only at sight of the Countess Croy that my proud mask fell. Without greeting her, I buried my face in both hands in order to show my contempt for her deception. Gently but firmly she drew my hands from my face and said, "Look at me, dear child! I've come here because of a wish of His Majesty." Then she informed me that the Emperor had expressed a wish to speak to the one lady who was present when his *très chère tante et mère* had spoken her last words. I do not know what I replied, truly I do not. It was as though an earthquake had shaken me up inside, throwing off the stones from the graves of my lost hopes. The Emperor wanted to know the last words of the Lady Regent. No one could fulfill his wish except myself. I would see him again: I would see him in spite of everyone! He himself—the Emperor—commanded it!

Suddenly I heard the Countess Croy saying: "No, you do not understand me, Arabella. We cannot permit this interview, for there is no one at the Court who does not know why you had to leave Valladolid that time. The Emperor himself will not insist on this interview once he knows the name of the lady. Will you at last confide to me the last words of Her Highness so that I may be able to pass them on to the Emperor in your place."

Instantly I replied: "No, I will not do that!" And I kept my word; for now it seemed I held a talisman in my grasp. She tried to wrest it from me, but I remained firm. To every entreaty I replied triumphantly that I would confide the words only to the Emperor himself.

The Countess was in despair. "Do understand, my child," she implored me, "that it is not a matter of you but of the unimpeachable name of the sovereign. Ah, if only you had followed my advice and taken your vows as a nun!"

At these words a daring idea came into my mind. "Would I be allowed to speak to His Majesty if I were a nun?" I asked.

"If you took religious vows," she replied hesitantly, "it would certainly help towards silencing the many rumors which have been going about. And I myself know that even when you were in Valladolid His Majesty wished something of the kind."

And now, Reverend Mother, you probably expect I should have had a severe spiritual struggle. But it was not like that at all. I had not a moment's struggle with myself, not one moment's. From the very beginning I had made up my mind without question. A little old mirror which the good nuns had put up as a concession to the youthful vanity of their guest shone on the wall in front of me. I can still see my sly little face in the shining glass as I told the poor Countess straight out that I had decided to take her advice. In fact, I was cunning enough to assert that my stay with the good nuns had won me over to a liking for convent life, and without the flicker of an eyelid I declared that I was ready to ratify my decision by taking my vows at once.

She looked extremely surprised but made no objection to my suggestion. Was I really deceiving her, or did she only wish to be deceived? Ah, it was a long time now since she had slept with her eyes open. Since the Lady Regent's death she had really become a short-sighted old woman. Besides, she had been longing for me to take vows. In short, she believed me. Later I heard that there were others behind her at that moment for whom this alleged decision of mine was unquestionably most opportune. And so my vow was accepted. I solemnly bound myself to enter the religious life although I had no intention of keeping that promise. On the contrary, what I did, I did solely in order to oblige people to allow me to see the Emperor again. I had one desire in doing so—to respond to the loving look which had previously rested on me. I had no aim beyond this. Hence my vow was a complete deception, in fact, a sacrilege, and my only excuse for this was the inexcusable readiness of those who permitted that overhasty act. Ah, they were only too happy to permit it—for his sake. A few days later the Countess accompanied me back to the Regency, where I was to have the interview with His Majesty in the former audience chamber of Her Highness.

*

As I entered the room a slim male figure stood up and advanced a few steps towards me. I heard a somewhat repressed voice say: "Donna Arabella, permit me to express due reverence for your future state." I found myself being led to an armchair and being asked to sit down. The Emperor sat down in front of me on the Lady Regent's chair. But I could not fully perceive his face, for I was as if suddenly struck blind—the sheer rapture of being near him had robbed me of all my strength. I only knew that the glance for which I had almost pined away with longing must be resting on me now.

Trembling, I raised my eyes, and as I did so I felt all the desire, and all the ardor and all the devotion of my heart rush to my eyes, presenting themselves to the eyes of the other joyously, without condition and without reserve. For only one single second did I feel this. Then my glance staggered back: I had now seen fully the face in front of me. But how unspeakably it had changed! How empty it had become! Oh, how much it had lost in those few years of ruling! True, it was still the same pale aristocratic face with the slight protruding underlip . . . terribly young . . . too terribly young for an Emperor—and all the time so terribly lonely! But this loneliness was no longer like an open gate inviting entrance. It was turned in upon itself,

raised, as it were, from its own depths, accepted and trans-
formed, as a gentle, nostalgic landscape is changed into one
that is noble when a castle with massive walls is built from
the stones of its hills and finally dominates the natural
landscape far and wide. . . . Not a tremor of the slender
hand which rested on the arm of the high chair, not a
flicker of the fair eyelashes betrayed the agitation of my
memory. And that glance of hidden passion which had
once cried out and to which I had dreamed of responding
those many days and nights—that glance was no longer
there. Nothing was there now but the glance of the Emperor. I was confronted by something utterly inaccessible,
the absolute inapproachability of pure majesty! It was as
though I were falling into an abyss. For the first time I
understood what the Empire meant.

The Emperor, in his subdued voice, was addressing me a
second time. "Donna Arabella, we congratulate you on
your decision to take the veil. The crisis which is facing
western Christendom at present calls for much prayer. We
are grateful for the opportunity of commending ourselves
and our Empire to your prayers."

Again I felt swallowed up in an abyss. So the Emperor
really believed that I wished to take the veil! And he had
to believe it, for I had shamefully deceived him as I had all
the others. In my frenzy I had not been conscious of this
hitherto. Now the deceptions I had practiced descended on
my spirit like a mist. I was overwhelmed with burning
shame, a feeling of deep unworthiness in face of the guile-
lessness of this young Emperor: the pain of his coldness

was almost a balm compared with the pain his contempt would cause me. And yet I felt that this would be inescapable if my deception came to light.

Now there was only one way I could save myself. I must make the lie come true, I must acknowledge my vow, I must fulfill it. But how frightful that would be! The cold, dead air of the convent! And oh, the unceasing round of prayer day and night. The thought of being buried alive like that! Who could give me the strength to go through with it? Only this man before me, but he was now wholly and solely an emperor, nothing more—I had nothing but pure majesty to cling to now. And now this Majesty was waiting for my answer. I had to make my decision.

I was seized with the wild courage of despair. Yes, there was no one there now but an emperor. But could one not love even an emperor? Could one not do that even behind convent walls? Yes, one could do that. Now the majesty of my own heart began, now I was his equal—and that was what I wished to be.

"Not only my prayers but my whole future life as a nun shall be a constant sacrifice for Your Majesty and Your Majesty's realm."

I had come out with it. I had as it were repeated my vow, and this time it was irrevocable! This time it was a perpetual vow and I would have to keep it to the end of my life!

The Emperor remained silent. Had the vehemence of my answer struck him dumb? The lonely young face in front of me remained impenetrable.

And now the slight figure leaning back in the chair drew itself erect. Quite suddenly His Majesty turned to the real object of the interview. I heard him asking: "Have we been rightly informed, Donna Arabella, that you were present when the Lady Regent dictated that farewell letter to us which concluded with the request that we should complete her work on the Church at Brou?"

I replied that this was so. The Emperor hesitated for a moment as if he were searching for words which were not immediately at his command. There was something noble in this hesitation, and I understood that he wished to protect the dead lady's secret. At last he almost blurted out: "We wish to know above all what Her Highness meant by this request, for there is a sentence missing in the letter. What impression did you get regarding Her Highness's last moments?"

"Her Highness seemed to be dying like a saint," I replied.

The Emperor looked up with pleased surprise, but he cast down his eyes again before they could meet mine. "You believe then," he said, "that you understood from Her Highness. . . ." Again the repressed voice searched for the right words . . . "that she was submitting to the demand of the Church in one very important matter?" A tone of uneasiness, due, no doubt, to concern for the spiritual welfare of the beloved woman who had been a mother to him, came into the young Emperor's voice.

I was unable to answer at once. Did the last words of Her Highness really express that submission which the

Emperor meant? Indeed, did they not express, together with this submission, much more: the complete triumph of her love? But the Emperor was asking about her submission. First I had to recall her words. As you can guess, Reverend Mother, just these words had escaped the memory of your unruly daughter.

"Her Highness," I said hesitantly, "expressed the wish that the church in Brou should be given by Your Majesty the high altar which it still lacks."

"That is what I had hoped to learn from you," said the Emperor, visibly relieved. "Thank you very much. You have confirmed to me that Her Highness departed this life as a Christian princess and the daughter of an Emperor. And I hope, Donna Arabella, that your own departure from this world may also be a sacrifice offered to God in pure love." The Emperor seemed about to dismiss me.

I was paralyzed with horror. Was this all that I had purchased with my frightful vow? Was I to be buried alive my whole life long for the sake of this cold and formal interview? Once again my despairing passion flamed up. Yes, there was no one there now but an emperor, and one could love an emperor. Even an emperor could surely feel that there was a majesty of the heart—and he should be made to feel it.

"Sire," I burst out, "Her Highness's last words were: 'I love God, I have always loved Him, I have loved Him in His image—for there is only one love—God accepts every love as if it were offered to Himself.'" And now I lifted my lowered eyes and looked up to him. That look—the look I wanted with all my being to return. . . . Now, getting hold of my excitement, I looked into his eyes—into the Emperor's large eyes.

At my outburst he had turned very pale. Now that touching self-command mirrored in his young face faltered and gave way to an expression of mortal terror: I had replied to that glance of long ago and my reply had been understood. The man in him had grasped the kind of love my vow meant. A breathless, abysmal, silence threatened to engulf everything.

The Emperor had already stood up. Still deathly pale, he offered me his arm and graciously led me to the door. There the strictly ceremonial farewell took place in complete silence. I felt that this silence could never be broken again.

*

And yet it was to be broken. A few days later the Emperor's confessor arrived at the Convent of the Annunciation, to which I had returned with the Countess Croy immediately after the audience. In the facile words of a courtier, but with an undertone of fatherly benevolence, he informed me that His Majesty had received the impression that my dedication to the religious life had been undertaken in circumstances which were contrary to the requirements of complete spiritual freedom. His Majesty therefore offered to have my vows annulled by Rome and so make it possible for me to return to the world either as a lady in waiting to some noblewoman or, since I was an orphan, as adopted daughter of a noble family in my own country. Or, if I preferred it, a suitable marriage could be arranged for me. At this last proposal I started violently, and the priest tactfully dropped the subject. It was left to me to choose from these suggestions, he continued. In making them, His Majesty's sole thought was to give me back complete freedom regarding my future life. "So take courage, Donna Arabella," concluded the priest, "and do not be afraid to remedy a wrong decision. Step out confidently on the road which His Majesty wants to smooth for you; it is the one suitable for you."

Then something extraordinary happened to me. I found myself unable to take that road. What had happened? Had I not been shuddering with horror at the thought of being a nun? Had I not just returned from the audience with tormenting thoughts in my mind as to how my life was finished and the long night beginning? Instead it was a new day breaking. I would be free once more to swing myself on to the richly embossed saddle of a little Arab horse. I would be allowed to dance, play the lute, and adorn myself; to wear a wreath on my head and a ring on my finger like other brides! The world had lost all its sense and charm for me; it suddenly fell into the past behind me. Only one person meant anything to me. The Emperor. He who had given me back my lost freedom. Everyone else had been intent only on fettering me. Everyone else had regarded me only as a foolish child, but he had taken my part as if I were his equal and a person worthy of freedom. Long ago he had wanted to send the dreaming girl into a convent, but he so respected the awakened woman who loved him that he left her free to decide for herself. I felt that this was indeed the greatest thing which he could grant me. Yes, my life was beginning again, and just when I thought it was ending. Now I was capable of living only for the Emperor, and where could I do that except behind convent walls?

"Monsignor," I said, radiant with joy, "please convey my grateful thanks to His Majesty for his noble and generous offer. But I have made my choice once more. In full freedom I repeat the answer which I have already given to His Majesty: my future religious life shall be a constant sacrifice for His Majesty and His Majesty's realm."

The priest gave me a long and searching look. He had a skeptical but not an unbelieving countenance; much knowledge of man and much doubt of him seemed engraved on it. There was nothing ignoble in his expression.

"I shall not try to persuade you to change your mind, Donna Arabella," he said at last, "for it would be to no purpose. I know that human love also can prove to be a way to God. That is what the great Master Plato taught us. The Empire and its rulers have need for interceding hands, for the course of the world is not regulated alone by man. Therefore dedicate yourself to representing His Majesty before God. I shall inform him of your decision; whether His Majesty will accept it, I do not know. But do not expect any answer."

With this he gave me his blessing and left.

Reverend Mother, you already know most of what I still have to write. Almost immediately after that interview I formally entered the Order of the Annunciation, to whose care, as I have already said, the mortal remains of the Lady Regent had been entrusted awaiting the transfer to Brou. When this transfer took place I was already wearing the veil of a novice, and according to the Rule of the Order I would no longer have been allowed to leave the Enclosure. But something highly unusual happened. To my utter astonishment my superiors gave me permission to accompany the beloved remains to Brou. You were Superior General at the time, Reverend Mother, and on making your visitation to our convent, you yourself brought me the dispensation from the bishop. This had no doubt been obtained at the request of someone of high position, although the reason given read that it was the due of the illustrious deceased to be accompanied to her tomb not only by the Deputies of the Estates, but also by one of her former ladies in waiting, and that this lady should be the one whom the Lady Regent herself had intended should accompany her to Brou.

Thus I entered the world once more in order to share the last sad journey of my former mistress. You have already seen the official account of it, Reverend Mother.

On arrival in Brou we learned that the church was first to be consecrated; the high altar, given by His Majesty, had now been erected. Numerous important persons were expected for the burial, but the consecration was to be performed as quietly as possible and with only the most necessary witnesses. It was naturally desired that the belated consecration should not attract the public eye for fear of reawakening certain rumors concerning the Lady Regent which were best forgotten. Originally the Emperor himself had been expected in Brou, but then we heard that difficult State business prevented his coming and that he could only send a deputy, whose name was not mentioned.

Count van Hoogstraten, the leading Deputy, and I set off for the church at an early hour in the morning. Two priests were waiting for us at the door, and they silently conducted us up the aisle. The main body of the church was deserted but the procession of the consecrating bishop and his accompanying priests was moving along by the sides where the consecration crosses were set into the walls. We entered the choir where the two priests showed us to our places. Mine was covered with a red cloth, and a red cushion lay on the floor. But I hardly noticed these adornments, so deeply affected was I by the place, the sanctuary of my dead mistress's love, that love which had only found its completion in God. I thought of her dying words. Would they also apply to me one day: God accepts every love as if it were offered to Himself? Ah, it seemed that not even the Emperor accepted mine! As the priest had foretold, he had never answered me. Had my choice not pleased him? Had he declined to have the prayer and sacrifice of one who loved him here on earth plead for him before God? I did not know. But was it necessary to know? Was not my whole religious life based on that utter sacrifice which asks no certainty? And was not every truly great love always ready to give without return? No, there was no need for either certainty or answer.

The bishop, together with his clergy, had completed the various stages of the consecration. The church had been given to God. God entered into it! the Mass began, the first Mass in this house of God. I knelt down. As I did so my eyes rested, for the first time consciously on the adornment of my stall-chair—the red velvet which covered it bore the Imperial device. Only then did I realize that I was occupying the place originally intended for His Majesty. *I* was his unnamed deputy! Overwhelmed with emotion I bent down and kissed the words *Plus ultra.*

Reverend Mother, I have finished the account which you told me to write.

THE TOWER
OF THE CONSTANT

THE TOWER OF THE CONSTANT

THE Prince de Beauvau had arrived in Aigues-Mortes in a very bad humor. His exalted patroness, the all-powerful Marquise, had at last refused her consent to any further postponement of his depressing visit there. So he had set out with much reluctance for the god-forsaken little place, and had passed a sleepless night there, plagued by mosquitoes and oppressed by the spectral gloom of the landscape. In the morning he had attended Mass, as his office required of him, and now, accompanied by his chaplain, was on his way to visit the notorious Tower of the Constant, where the prisoners were kept.

The Prince had a natural aversion to the sight of human misery, and had largely succeeded up to the present in avoiding painful experiences of this kind. But the Marquise had insisted that in his new office as Governor of the *department* it was imperative that he carry out this duty, unpleasant though it might be.

"Do as I ask you, dear friend, while I'm still in a position to advise you," she had urged. "You will not have reason to regret it."

What did this curious word "still" mean? Was the lady afraid that she was losing her tender hold over the heart of the King? The Prince could not imagine this being so; nor could he see at all why the zealous patroness of Voltaire should make this matter her own. It was, after all, primarily the concern of the clergy. All the same, the fact that she did so was significant—so he gave way to her wish, though reluctantly.

*

He arrived on a depressing day of silver-gray melancholy. The sea, which in former times had lapped the walls of the town, had long since receded, and the harbour was silted up. Here, where the Crusaders of Saint Louis had once gone aboard their ships singing psalms, a pale swampy landscape now stretched as far as the eye could reach. White crystals—the salt left behind by the sea in its retreat—shimmered over this reedy grass desert, and it was this whiteness which gave to the landscape its singularly dead and spectral aspect. Was the sea too, in keeping with the changed times, seeking to break away from the proud past? Was it withdrawing from this region as the great historical happenings had withdrawn from it? The Prince did not put this question into words for he was listening, more than a little bored, to the suave voice of his chaplain, who was drawing his attention to the fact that the Albigensians and the Templars had been imprisoned in Aigues-Mortes too, and that in holding the Huguenots imprisoned here nowadays the King was following in the footsteps of Saint Louis. For the fight against heresy was the legitimate continuation of the Crusades.

It was with difficulty that the Prince suppressed a show of impatience, for like all the intelligentsia of Paris he was a convinced freethinker—a firm believer in pure reason and freedom of the spirit, in nature and humanitarianism. He was quite incapable of conceiving what was really meant by heresy: apparently in the heyday of the great Huguenot families it was the way to power and influence just as to persecute the Huguenots obviously was today.

Now they had come close up to the Tower of the Constant. It rose steep, windowless and frighteningly high into the silent silver-gray sky, as though it had consciously wrested itself free of the perverted landscape to gaze out on to the open sea. Had this tower, as its name implied, refused to move with the times, and was the chaplain therefore right when he asserted that its present use was in keeping with the high and noble spirit of the Crusades? Did not the summit of this tower still contain the Sanctuarium of St. Louis?

Their footsteps echoed loudly as they crossed the bridge over the moat full of stagnant water which encircled the tower. It smelled of seaweed and decayed fish, for though the summit of this tower greeted the open sea, its foundations stood deep in the swampy soil of this god-forsaken region.

The visitors were received at the other side of the bridge by the still youthful commandant of the Tower—he had recently succeeded his deceased father in the office. To the

Prince he handed a list of the prisoners. It consisted solely of female names. "The men are on the galleys," explained the young commandant. "We get only an occasional one here who's too weak for that service."

The Prince glanced down the long line of names: a cross beside some of them indicated that the bearers had already died. "To what terms of imprisonment are these people condemned?" he asked.

The young commandant looked at him astonished. Did the Prince not know that the years are forgotten here?

"We have received no orders about that, my Prince," he replied. A little timidly he added, "We have been hoping to receive some from you." His gentle, almost boyish face, showed a sympathy which he dared not express. It was dangerous to be on the side of the prisoners at Aigues-Mortes.

The Prince understood the unspoken appeal. "That will depend on the reception my chaplain receives here," he said. "He has orders to address the prisoners. I myself do not wish to have any contact with them. There must not be any scenes. I cannot have the ladies falling on their knees before me and pleading for mercy. So you will please avoid addressing me in the presence of the prisoners."

The young commandant bowed silently. He had already noted that the Prince had refrained from wearing any sign of his rank and office.

Now they began to climb the narrow winding stairs; the endless steps gave the Prince the impression that he was in a giant shell which had been spat out from the sea. As the spirals grew more and more narrow, he felt smothered. Yet, he wished that these stairs would never come to an end, so agonizing was his dread of the sight which awaited him at the top.

While lost in the agony of his thoughts, the terrible moment arrived. The young commandant opened a heavily barred and bolted door, and they entered a great circular room. At first, it seemed almost in darkness, for there were no windows, only a few slits. Unspeakably stale and foul air overwhelmed the nostrils of the visitors. The Prince, accustomed only to the delicate perfumes of the Court, felt nauseous. Slowly, as his eyes grew accustomed to the half light, he made out a small group of women huddled close together. They were all dressed in old and faded garments, and their faces were faded and old . . . white faces, as if they were survivors of an age long past, or more, living corpses. Involuntarily he thought of the deposit left by the sea . . . had the bitter salt of these women's tears left their faces marked as the retreating sea had marked the landscape outside?

"Here are the prisoners," said the young commandant, presenting them and giving the name and age of each. There were many women of over sixty among them, but to judge by appearances, the Prince would have thought that nearly all of them were very much older than that.

The chaplain was asking each prisoner whether she abjured her heresy and was prepared to return to the bosom of the Church. All remained silent. It was not even certain that they were capable of grasping the meaning of the words. The chaplain repeated his question, but this time, instead of saying the bosom of the Church, he inadvertently said "freedom."

At first there was deep silence as before. Then suddenly two of the wretched creatures clasped each other's hands as if for mutual encouragement. At the same time a crazy, tremulous, almost insane joy distorted their agonized faces. Then hand in hand they staggered towards the chaplain. But before they could utter a word a very frail, yet very clear, voice called out from the back of the room: *Résistez!* The two women stood still and burst into tears.

The priest scowled. This was the expected resistance. "Whose voice was that?" he asked angrily.

"Her name is Marie Durand," said the commandant. "She's very ill," he added apologetically. "No doubt she speaks in fever."

"All the same she seems to be the soul of the resistance here," replied the chaplain.

The youthful face of the commandant betrayed growing anxiety. "This resistance has two sides, Monsieur l'Abbé," he said, "for Marie Durand has a very happy gift of comforting the prisoners. The new arrivals in particular—she often saves them from despair. My God, you have no idea," he blurted out, "you have no idea how frightful these outbreaks are. . . . Just think, just think. . . ."

"Very well then, conduct me to your protégée," the chaplain cut him short. "I'm bound in duty to carry out my task here."

They entered an alcove even darker and more vile in

smell than the main room. An old woman, obviously very ill, was lying on a filthy straw matress. The wretchedness which the Prince had already seen was unimaginably terrible, but the sight that met his eyes here was still worse.

"My God, my God," he murmured, covering his face with his hands.

The chaplain was asking the sick woman whether it was she who had cried *"Résistez!"* But now something completely unexpected happened. The woman sat up and, taking no notice of the chaplain's question, she stretched out her withered old hand to the Prince. "Welcome!" she cried; her voice as before was feeble but very clear. "Welcome, and have no fear, for it is good to be here!"

Her words seemed to come from another world, and under the circumstances, seemed so completely incomprehensible they remained unanswered. What moved Marie Durand to utter them can never be explained. Did she take the Prince to be a newly arrived prisoner, one of those men rejected for the galleys, or did she only want to banish his horror at the sight of her own misery? Did she perhaps think that she must console him in his hour of trial as she had consoled so many before? One thing alone was certain: that this most pitiable woman was sorry for him.

"No, do not doubt me," she continued. "Many have come here in despair, but none have remained completely without comfort. The good God loves prisoners. He gives them inner freedom. He will give it to you too. Oh, the freedom of the spirit is invincible. No tower, no gate, however firmly locked, can destroy it!"

79

Meanwhile the Prince stood there as if paralyzed. He felt that his whole former world was falling to pieces. Suddenly he seemed to be standing on the summit of the tower, looking out at the sea. . . .

"How long have you been here?" he managed to ask at last.

"I don't know," she replied in a friendly voice, "the time has gone so quickly—it has no importance here. It's almost as though it no longer existed. Eternity begins in this tower." And she smiled.

"Marie Durand has been here thirty-nine years," the young commandant quickly replied. He observed with hope how shattered the Prince was. "She was very young when they brought her here. My father often told me about it. She was hardly more than a child, rosy-cheeked and fresh as a little apple. That's how my father used to describe her. But then, that was thirty-nine years ago. . . ."

"Thirty-nine years! Thirty-nine years!" repeated the Prince. And as he spoke the words his face grew pale, matching the palor of the prisoners.

"Do you wish us to go?"' asked the commandant, for he feared that the Prince might faint.

The Prince made no answer. Suddenly he bent down over the withered worn old hand before him and kissed it reverently. "Marie Durand, you are free," he said. "You are free from this moment." Then, turning to the young commandant: "They are all free. I command you to release them all this very day."

Then he hurried out of the room and down the stairs.

The chaplain only caught up to him down on the bridge. "For God's sake, my Prince, allow me to take your arm," he said. You can hardly stand."

"On the contrary, Monsieur l'Abbé," replied the Prince, "I have only now got a firm foothold—for I have lost my faith."

The chaplain started. "So you had a faith to lose, my Prince?" he said with some irony. "I did not know that."

"Yes, indeed, I had a faith to lose," retorted the Prince. "I believed in the triumph of atheism."

The chaplain was slightly startled, but he replied suavely, "This is a very good thing, my Prince. The ways of God with a soul are often wonderful, but for the moment let us think of the ways of man. You were so merciful as to order the immediate release of the prisoners. The commandant asks that you let him have the necessary letter of authority from the King."

These words gave the Prince a shock. Only now did he realize that he had overstepped his powers: the release of prisoners was the prerogative of the King. On the other hand, the order which he had given could not be cancelled on any account. His authority as governor of the region was at stake here.

"The commandant has only to carry out my orders," he said, his words edged with contempt. The royal letter of authority is my affair. It will be handed over in time." And when the chaplain still seemed dubious, he continued: "The commandant has my word of honor."

A few hours later the Prince was on his way to Paris, this time alone. The chaplain was following in another carriage, as the Prince, who was still deeply shaken by his experience with the prisoners, would have found any company intolerable. Moreover, he was slightly uneasy concerning the royal letter of authority which had to be procured at once, because he knew reluctantly how His Majesty was to grant audiences in a hurry. He knew only too well what it meant to wait in numerous ante-rooms expecting to get the King's ear. There was no time for all this. The Prince was determined to keep his pledged word, no matter what difficulties stood in his way.

"Reinette will know what to do," he consoled himself, involuntarily calling his powerful patroness by the charming petname of her girlhood, which had proved to be in a sense prophetic. Reinette had in fact become a "little queen," or rather, a great queen. After all, what was the sovereign's consort compared with his powerful *maitresse?* A shadow, a nonentity, the bearer of a mere title. Yes, to be sure, the manner of Reinette's rise to power had caused the Prince much grief at first; it had been no easy matter for him to surrender his beloved to the King. He was often tempted to assume the role of the Marquis of Montespan, who had once appeared at the court of *Le Roi Soleil* in mourning when the King had taken his wife from him and raised her to the rank of royal mistress. But the Prince had not appeared in mourning—times had changed. Today even the greatest families deemed it an honor to provide royal mistresses. After all, one was a child of one's time.

One only made oneself ridiculous if one did not fall into step. And Reinette herself had taken pains to console her discarded lover. With gentle hands and quiet judgment she had successfully assuaged his wounded pride.

"Now I shall be able to look after you at last," she had said to him. "You will no longer be the uninfluential bearer of your great name. You will attain the position that is due to you at last, and this, just this, will be my one real happiness in my life by the King's side."

She had kept her word. As Reinette's protégé he had climbed the steep ladder of success which had led to the high office he now held. He had accepted all this without resistance. In fact a truly remarkable state of harmony between himself and Reinette had come into being—a state of harmony which he had never been able to explain to himself. But today for the first time he had become conscious of a slight uneasiness as if false cards had somehow been played in this matter. Of course, so he persuaded himself, this uneasiness was only due to the immense urgency of his present need.

Dawn was breaking as the Prince arrived in Paris after a breakneck journey. Even since he had become governor of that distant region he had continud to reside in the capital. In fact he was wont to assert in all seriousness that a man like himself could not live elsewhere. While still on his way to Paris he had sent a horseman on ahead with a billet so that the Marquise should be prepared for his request.

On arriving he hurriedly shook off the dust of the

journey, changed his clothes, and set out without delay for Versailles in order to see the lady at her *levée,* that charming scene at which the numerous followers and petitioners of the mighty favorite foregathered each morning.

The Prince could hardly wait to get to her apartments. But when the delicate perfume of his former lady—a perfume which ordinarily enchanted him—met his nostrils on the threshold, he suddenly felt that extraordinarily strong disquietude again. For a moment he hesitated on the threshold, but the lackey flung open the doors all too promptly to the familiar visitor.

The Marquise was sitting at her dressing table having her hair dressed. She was wearing an exquisite low cut negligée which left her beautiful shapely arms bare. As the morning was dull, candles had been lit. They poured their warm golden radiance over the whole room full of people, who were pressing half impatiently, half tenderly around the much courted lady. Some, coveting the privilege of helping in the toilet of the mighty one, were handing her maid the hairpins. Others, standing about in the background, were holding written petitions in their hands and waiting for a sign from the Marquise to hand them to her. But the lady seemed completely absorbed in the adornment of her person. With her eyes fixed on the large ebony-framed mirror which a kneeling maid was holding up to her, she smiled at her own reflection but took no notice at all of the guests who had come to her *levée.*

The Prince, who had remained by the door struggling with his strange uneasiness, also failed to catch her attention at first. Although the Marquise was surrounded by all possible manner of admirers, a strange image, and one which had already come to him momentarily several times before, sprang to his mind at sight of her—a picture or vision, as it were, of one of those beautiful and shimmering reptiles that are said to dance all alone in the moonlight for their own pleasure. But this image was a highly illusory and imaginative one, for the Marquise was anything but a lonely person. Nevertheless, it seemed to have some decided relation to reality.

Meanwhile the voice of the lackey who had opened the door to the Prince was heard announcing the name of the latest arrival. The Marquise turned round and an expression of joyful astonishment spread over her face.

"So you're safe back, Prince!" she cried, stretching out both hands—those very small, remarkably strongly formed hands—to him. But before he could bend to kiss them her faced changed. The joyful smile faded, the eyes—those very clever, very observant eyes of hers—looked at the Prince with displeased surprise. Yes, almost with anger. It suddenly seemed to him that she shared his uneasiness, or at least had become aware of it in some mysterious way. But this lasted only for a few seconds; then the Marquise assumed her joyful vivacious smile once more.

"I'm glad to see you back, dear Prince," she said with that unmatched graceful assurance of hers, "but I see that that journey has taken a great deal out of you. . . ."

Again her face assumed an expression of slight wonderment. Suddenly she stood up and said, "The *levée* is at an end; I thank you. Good-bye all of you until tomorrow morning."

At her words everyone, with the exception of the Prince, withdrew. The longed-for moment had come; he was alone before his patroness.

She looked at him with anxious eyes. "My poor friend," she said once more. "What a lot this journey has taken out of you! But it was really necessary in order to improve your position in certain circles. As a freethinker you are not in the habit of taking these circles very seriously, but believe me, they are most influential. And now let's say no more about that journey of yours," she continued gaily. "Look instead at this delightful gift which someone has given me."

Saying this she went to a little glass case, took out a delicately carved ivory crucifix, and handed it to the Prince. "The Reverend Mother Prioress of St. Cyr honored me with this present," she said. "So you see my position too has improved—in certain circles."

The Prince already knew about the Marquise's latest pastime: the practice of piety. She was to be found reading books of devotion; she collected holy pictures, and she visited nuns. He knew what all this meant: she was trying to obtain Absolution which, as the King's mistress, she had been denied for years. But why did she want it? Had she too not been a disciple of Voltaire for many years past. What, after all, could the Church's Absolution mean to her?

Well, she simply wanted to be favored in all quarters,

the Prince told himself with an indulgent smile. It was just one more small, perhaps rather lovable vanity, a formality which would enable her to appear at the Communion rail as a pious woman whose esteem in the eyes of the Church could not be impaired, even by adultery. The Prince had up till now only smiled tolerantly over the religious aspirations of his friend. Today, however, he recoiled with horror when her little hand, laden with costly rings, showed him the crucifix. He looked away; and suddenly the image of Marie Durand was before him. What a different impression a crucifix would convey in her hand!

For a moment both fell silent, then the Prince pulled himself together, remembering that after all he was here to ask for an urgent audience with the King. Had the Marquise not received his note? Quickly and without any preliminaries he said, "Reinette, may I ask if you've done anything about my audience with the King?"

The beautiful lady's clever eyes became impenetrable. "And why do you require this urgent audience, my friend?" she asked coolly.

Suddenly he was overwhelmed with the conviction that she already knew what was forcing him to his request. But how could this be possible? Had she read from his face what he had experienced in Aigues-Mortes? Did she not only sense the alteration in their relations but also possess the key to its meaning? Once more his experience in Aigues-Mortes came so strongly into his consciousness that he was convinced Reinette read it from his face.

She shook her head, with its finely powdered coiffure.

No, she knew nothing at all; yet, she was in the habit of looking at things, shrewdly.

In spite of her surface charm he clearly perceived her growing wariness. Oh, she knew him too well. It was impossible to try to hide anything from her.

"Stand by me, Reinette," he pleaded helplessly. "I must speak to the King."

Those clever eyes looked at him more and more cautiously while her mouth yielded to a smile. Not convulsively. Oh, no. Her command over those generously painted lips was complete and superb. Obviously it was clear to her that a change had taken place in him, and she was searching out its cause.

"Have you committed some folly or other in Aigues-Mortes, my friend?" she asked lightly, in an effort to joke it off. No, there was definitely no point in trying to hide things from her!

"On the contrary," he replied indignantly, "I have done the only reasonable thing that was to be done there: I have ordered that the unfortunate prisoners be released at once. But I did not have the necessary authority from the King to do so."

For a few moments there was an overwhelming silence. The Prince sensed the Marquise turning pale under her heavy make-up.

"So. You want to land in the tower of Aigues-Mortes yourself, it seems?" she said with a short laugh.

He tried to smile too, for surely what she hinted at was sheer nonsense.

"I simply must safeguard the young commandant," he said, ignoring the question. "I gave him my word of honor that he would receive the royal letter of authority in time."

Again the Marquise shook her beautiful head, this time in disapproval. "I gather that you want to ask His Majesty's approval of the release of the prisoners which you have already effected?" she asked. "But do you realize what that means?"

"I realize, Reinette, that you can do anything with His Majesty," he replied.

Again she laughed her short low laugh. "That's true, my friend," she said, "but you forget that I'm most . . . *most* . . . anxious to obtain Absolution. You can see why I definitely cannot approach His Majesty just now to ask for an amnesty for . . . heretics."

He was overcome with repugnance for her religious aspirations. Once more the picture of Marie Durand thrust itself before him. Two immeasurably different kinds of piety stood sharply opposed: the sacrifice of silent, almost joyful resignation, devoid of all the comfort of a church; and, the ambitious craving of a vain woman for ecclesiastical recognition, coveted as though it were a special object of adornment. For a moment he felt tempted to renounce the lady's intercession. But he could not bring himself to do it—his need was too urgent.

"If you don't help me, Reinette," his voice rose excitedly, "my young subordinate is lost. Surely you cannot force me to break my word of honor to him?"

The Marquise had recovered from her shock. "Calm

yourself," she said. "It is true, I cannot ask for an audience for you at the moment, but go to Pére Laroche from me and tell him candidly what happened in Aigues-Mortes. If there is anyone who can settle the matter for you with the King, it is he. But hurry before the affair is noised about."

The Prince stood up. Actually he now experienced a curious sense of relief that the Marquise had refused to intercede for him with the King, though he felt a strong repugnance towards the priest too. The priest belonged to the Jesuit Order, and the Jesuits were not only strong opponents of the Prince's liberal friends but also notoriously inimical to the Huguenots. But he dared not let these considerations hold him back now.

Accordingly he called on the priest, who received him with the urban politeness of a man of the world and without any visible surprise. The Prince handed him the note which the Marquise had given him to present as a letter of introduction. Pére Laroche broke the seal and read half aloud, "Filled with deep anxiety for the preservation of our holy Faith, and overjoyed at being able to do Holy Church a little service. . . ."

The priest stopped and laughed aloud. "Aha, there she goes again at the same old tune, Madame la Marquise!" he cried, visibly amused. It sounded as if he meant: There she is, trying to pull wool over my eyes again! Then, having read the letter in silence to an end, he said: "You're certainly in a very difficult situation, Prince. Has Madame la Marquise been unable to promise you anything at all, then?"

"She promised me your help, that was all," replied the Prince in an irritated tone.

A half-ironical, half-tolerant smile flitted over the priest's face. It was a still youthful face, with its resolute features but so disciplined that in spite of its apparent candor of expression, it was practically impenetrable.

"Ah, yes, Madame la Marquise," he said with a sigh. "When she takes something into her head it's impossible to get it out of it."

Though no explanation followed, the Prince had the distinct impression that his patroness, in sending him to Father Laroche, had hoped to further her chance of obtaining Absolution from the latter, and that the priest had grasped this quite clearly although he did not betray the fact by a single word. Silently following the Marquise's note he said: "You yourself feel drawn to the Protestant faith, do you not?"

"No, on the contrary, I'm a freethinker, but the prisoners of Aigues-Mortes have made me see what a devout faith means," replied the Prince. In spite of his dangerous and painful situation he felt an exasperated temptation to emphasize to the Jesuit how deeply the attitude of the heretics had impressed him.

The priest perceived the challenge, but his imperturbable calm remained unruffled. "And what precisely was the wording of the order which you left behind in Aigues-Mortes?" he asked in a matter-of-fact tone.

The Prince felt a strong urge to shake the urbane courtesy of the Jesuit. "As Governor of the department, I ordered that the unfortunate prisoners be released forthwith," he said haughtily, feeling a momentary relish at the triumph of his powerful position. But the priest did not gratify him by showing horror, as the Marquise had done.

"That was very understandable, Prince," he said benevolently, "very understandable indeed from the humane point of view. I appreciate your attitude completely." Then, with the shadow of a smile, he continued: "We Jesuits have learned something useful from the latest intellectual trends. This rationalism, disastrous though its effects on orthodoxy may be, simply had to come—the Church could not cope alone with fanaticism."

The Prince listened with growing surprise as the priest continued in his frank way: "Well, I duly respect the order you gave in Aigues-Mortes, Prince, but of course it cannot be carried out in the absence of the royal mandate."

"But it *has* been carried out," said the Prince, emphatically. He was now conscious of a growing satisfaction in owning up to his arbitrary action, and once more savored the triumph of his position. "The young commandant carried out my order as a matter of course; he only required my promise that the royal mandate should follow later."

"And are you so sure that you will obtain this belated letter of authority by an audience with the King?" asked the priest.

"Why not?" replied the Prince obstinately. "The King is not a bigot. . . ." He deliberately chose this word, but the priest passed over this too with the same calm as before, and actually repeated the words.

"No, the King is not a bigot," he said, "but he has certain religious obligations. His coronation oath binds him to destroy heresy. You forget, Prince, that the persecution of your protégées is less the work of the Church than that of the State, which is striving to enforce uniformity of belief on the whole nation." After a moment's hesitation he continued: "As I said already, Prince, you are in a difficult position. I am less uneasy for the commandant than for you, for he merely executed the order of his superior, whereas you exceeded that of your superior. I fear we must reckon with your having to stand trial for this."

At the Jesuit's words the Prince felt as if he were being pushed with great suddenness into some place of primeval darkness from which there was absolutely no way out, and whose menacing existence he had deliberately ignored up till now. Anxiety for his young subordinate was still occupying his mind exclusively; the profound consciousness of his noble name and exalted position had preserved his confidence in his own safety. But now those jocose words of the Marquise, "So you want to land in the tower of Aigues-Mortes yourself, it seems!" suddenly registered in his consciousness as a fearful possibility.

No, the Prince de Beauvau was no hero. He was a delicately perceptive aristocrat, accustomed to the discreet language of courtiers, and to the beautiful sensitive ideas of his liberal friends. He had striven only for success and had always put the privileges of his class before any sacrifice, even the smallest one. The possibility indicated by the priest filled him with the same nameless horror which he had felt at the sight of the wretched prisoner, Marie Durand. Now this horror concerned himself and his own possible fate. He knew that the possibility which the priest had voiced had a very real basis. Had not a number of noblemen been tried and condemned only a few years ago because they had been convicted of listening to a Protestant preacher? Even if his noble rank saved him from being condemned to the galleys, it would not save him from imprisonment, perhaps in Vincennes, perhaps in Besançon, perhaps even in the Tower of the Constant in Aigues-Mortes. Actually, he had felt that within himself all the time, but had managed successfully to repel the thought each time it momentarily crossed his mind. Now his life, which until recently had had for its stage only the courtly splendour of Versailles, seemed to shift into the melancholy landscape of Aigues-Mortes which had so horrified him from the very first moment. He saw that scene stretched before him in its measureless desolation, the landscape covered with the dried salt tears of the sea which had fled unceasingly from that shore into its own inviolable freedom. In mounting the tower of Aigues-Mortes he had entered into another world from which there was no return.

The profound shock which the man before him was suffering had not escaped the priest. "All the same, it is naturally advisable to inform the King," he said, "and it seems to me that the Marquise is the only suitable person to make a plea for a royal pardon, not for the unhappy prisoners, for unfortunately that would be hopeless, but for you."

He stopped short because the Prince, whose face wore an indescribable expression, was shaking his head.

"I understand," said the priest. "You don't believe that the Marquise is willing to help. And actually I admit that she has other things on her mind just now, and the moment is not favorable for your purpose." He refrained from being more explicit, but of course the Prince had realized from the outset what he was referring to.

"Could you not give the Marquise her Absolution, Father?" he burst out, unable to control his agitation any longer. "Then her hands would be free!"

The priest shook his head with almost boyish vehemence. "Yes, if Madame la Marquise is prepared to leave Versailles for ever," he replied, smiling. "Otherwise not. For morals are as much above discussion as faith is. However, it is precisely their absence here which gives you your chance, Prince; I mean that it gives to the Marquise a power which is probably the only thing that could influence the King to a milder interpretation of his coronation oath. Naturally only in relation to you, not to the prisoners, I repeat. And, if I am correctly informed, you have already availed yourself of this power several times."

He stopped short again, for clearly there was something unexpected going on in the Prince's mind. "Do you perchance feel a repugnance towards engaging the help of Madame la Marquise?" he asked, astonished.

The Prince remained silent for a few moments. "Yes, I

have a very great objection," he answered at last in a choking voice. What he had only sensed vaguely until now had suddenly become absolute certainty: the shadow of Aigues-Mortes had even been cast upon his relations with the Marquise. That uneasy feeling which had come over him momentarily on entering her apartments—no, actually in the carriage on the way back to Paris—broke in upon his consciousness with magnified clarity now. He could not, he dared not ever again ask this woman to mediate for him.

The Jesuit, who was standing before him with downcast eyes, looked up with a swift searching glance. "I see," he said with quick perception, "your experience at Aigues-Mortes has not only shaken your heart and your feelings: it has also changed your soul. You prefer to trust to the good God. . . ."

He stopped, for the Prince, who felt he was already helplessly delivered up to a trial which would slowly but surely rob him of every hope, had covered his face with his hands.

For a moment there was silence between the two men. Then the Prince said, "No, that's just what I can't do. In Aigues-Mortes I lost my faith—my faith in atheism. I came to realize that there is still a Christian faith. But I myself am far from that faith." Then, with desperate resolve, he added, "So I must speak to the King. Father, is there any chance that you—I mean your Order—would save me?"

The priest looked at the Prince with sincere sympathy. "My advice to you would be to leave the country, and at once," he said. "Your chaplain was with you at Aigues-

Mortes. No one can blame him if he informs his ecclesiastical superiors of what you did. And you yourself are aware, Prince, of the attitude of our French hierarchy towards persons of other faiths, although nearly all our bishops play with the godless philosophy themselves. And yet, for a long while now these princes of the Church are not the persons in whose hands the final decision rests. I think you still fail to realize the true position, Prince. It is the power of the State which we have to deal with here."

The Prince could contain himself no longer. All the rumors which were current concerning the almost legendary power of the Jesuit Order sprang to his mind at this moment. "But what is the power of the State," he cried, "if the opinion of the mighty Order which you, Father, represent here, is in favor of tolerance?"

"Tolerance is not the policy of the Order which I represent," replied the Father, "and it never will be. But actually it is not a question of tolerance at all, but of something much nobler and deeper: it is a question of that humanity and mercy which one owes even to those whose belief one combats. But the hour of mercy has not yet struck in this country. It will come, perhaps in a hundred, perhaps not until two or three hundred years from now. Our present conversation here"—he smiled—"is set like a theatrical scene, so to speak, several centuries ahead of our time. These centuries will come, and when they come we shall be reproached most bitterly because of our prisoners. All those men chained to the galleys because of their faith are rowing the ship of Peter towards storms of accusation, and this despite the fact that the Holy Father has declared that the methods practiced today are not those of Christ and that our separated brethren should be led, not dragged, into the Church. Unfortunately however, our Church leaders, with their Gallic independence, do not feel obliged to listen to his fatherly voice."

"But after all, people say that your Order is so powerful and clever that it's able to achieve anything," persisted the Prince naively, for now he was positively clinging to the other as a last hope.

"No! Unfortunately there is nothing we can achieve," replied the priest, "not even a modest measure of moral order at the court of the 'Most Christian King,' as is clear from the case of Madame la Marquise which we have just been discussing. The fact is that we are no less endangered than you are, Prince. . . ." He hesitated for a moment, then continued with a smile, "As a matter of fact, our position is not at all unlike your own. There are formidable intrigues afoot—intrigues which reach even to Rome— and their purpose is to have our Order suppressed. I shall not be at all surprised if we too shall have to leave this country soon."

Once more the Prince was almost struck speechless with surprise. "So you people too are holding a lost position?" he asked slightly incredulously.

"Of course we are. The Christian is always defending a lost cause," replied the priest patiently. "And when you come to think of it, that's just as it should be. To man a lost position means to stand where Christ stood here on earth. The only danger for the Christian is that he may be tempted to clutch at the flag of this world to save himself."

The Prince looked at the priest helplessly. He could not understand his attitude. Did it spring from that famous detachment, that complete indifference in face of personal success or failure, with which the Jesuit Order was popularly credited?

"But after all I can only grasp the banner of this world," cried the Prince desperately, "because this world is very, very dear to me—it is the only one I have."

The Prince de Beauvau had reached the end of his control, and the priest looked at him with genuine concern; he was also making a swift mental assessment of the Prince's moral strength. As an experienced observer of human nature he noted that—humanly speaking—it was inadequate.

"Very well then," he said," let us try to save your world for you, Prince. But believe me, it can only be done through Madame la Marquise. Her power over the King is unlimited. It is she, not he, who is the real ruler of this country. One moment. . . ."

He scribbled a few lines on a sheet of paper and handed it to the Prince. Seeing the latter's hesitation, he added with a smile, "There's none of the intrigue you so obviously connect with Jesuits in these few lines. I am merely in the happy position of being able to assure Madame la Marquise that, contrary to her own opinion, she will be doing the Church—I mean, of course, the Church of the future— a service if she furthers your petition with the King."

*

The afternoon sun was already throwing its slanting rays into the streets of Paris as the Prince left the priest. He was in the most peculiar mood imaginable. He still felt an extraordinary repugnance towards his lady friend. Should he not first see what his enterprising philosopher friends could do for him? After all, it was said—indeed, admitted—that they had great influence with the higher clergy—and they should surely be glad to have an opportunity to put their theories of humanity into practice. He decided to drop into one of those elegant coffee-houses where many of them were to be found at this time of day.

And the Prince was lucky. As he entered the coffee-house no less than Monsieur Voltaire himself beckoned him to come and sit down at his table.

"How splendid that you've come, my dear Prince," he said. "I have been dying to talk with you. People are saying the most terrible things about you. Your chaplain is asserting that you played the role of Protestant martyr for the faith in Aigues-Mortes the other day. I half expected you to confront us Bible in hand the next time we'd see you!" As he said this an amused grin covered his uncomely face.

The Prince flushed. "And I expected that your circle, being converted by you to 'pure reason,' would be far too enlightened to believe such fairy-tales," he replied irascibly.

Monsieur Voltaire laughed his gnome-like laugh again. "I compliment you on your optimism, Prince," he replied malevolently, "But unfortunately I myself have come to the conclusion that reason is a beautiful if rare quality. I'm rather surprised if this didn't strike you in Aigues-Mortes. For the plight of your unfortunate prisoners is a sure proof that our influential contemporaries are lacking in all reason."

"Still more lacking in all humanity," replied the Prince. "And if I remember rightly, you, my esteemed friend, have often spoken in its favor. Therefore I trust I may appeal to your humanity now?"

"Good heavens, my dear Prince! Surely you don't wish to enlist my help to save you from the consequences of your action in Aigues-Mortes?" retorted the famous man with an exaggerated grimace. I have fallen into disfavor at Court, you know. They have actually had my book—my book, mark you—burned by the public hangman!"

The Prince stood up. He was clearly aware that these people could not or would not save him, for after all, he was definitely no longer one of them. For the first time he felt disappointed in the famous man whose faith in reason had been shaken when he himself had fallen into disfavor. What vanity! This man who was airing his intellectual views here in this cozy coffee-house, was he the same man who had once been his friend? How shoddy and superficial all this foppish intellectualism seemed when weighed against what he had seen in Aigues-Mortes—a burned book compared with the sacrifice of a whole life!

So, after all, Madame la Marquise represented the only chance left him. For the second time that day, he set off for Versailles; there was no time to lose. Monsieur Voltaire had made this evident by the fact that he already knew about his adventure in Aigues-Mortes.

Dusk was beginning to fall as his carriage drew up at the gate of the palace. The whole place was curiously silent and dark for such a comparatively early hour. The Prince was told that the card-party, which usually took place about this time, had been cancelled and that Madame la Marquise had already retired to her bedchamber. Nevertheless, he had himself announced at once.

The waiting maids were ceremoniously engaged in undressing their mistress as he entered the room. He immediately got the embarrassing impression that the Marquise was expecting the King, a prospect which filled him with acute discomfort. But at the same time he felt captivated by the bewildering enchantment of the room; the intimate objects lying around reminded him of those evenings when he himself was awaited by his beloved. A maid laid her lady's silk nightgown over the back of a gilded chair, then, having shaken up the pillows on the bed, withdrew discreetly on a sign from the Marquise. How well the Prince knew this sign, and with what tremulous expectation it had filled him in days gone by! Today it pierced him with a raging grief which momentarily drowned even the fear which had driven him here.

Meanwhile the lady carefully read the letter which the priest had given him for her. As she did so her face brightened visibly. Obviously the Father had found the right words. "Very well," she said, "I shall obtain the audience for you. I have to do what you and Father Laroche want," she added with a smile full of promise. Obviously she felt she was getting nearer to her own private aim.

But curiously enough this assurance did not relieve the Prince's spirits. "Reinette," he began uncertainly, "I often feel ashamed of your interceding with the King for me. Can you understand that?"

"No, I definitely cannot," she replied with a brusqueness which told him that she had guessed his thoughts. As she said this her face, from which the maids had removed the make-up, became visibly paler. The Prince felt a melancholy tenderness at the sight of her fading charms. And now he was seized with a longing to cast away all the possessions and honors which she had obtained for him. Was not his earthly love, after all, a precious jewel which should never be sacrificed for material success? He saw now that what he had gone through in Aigues-Mortes had touched even this domain of his life.

An uneasy silence fell between them.

At this moment a little clock on the mantelpiece struck the hour in a small childishly clear tone. The face of the Marquise assumed a tense listening expression. Steps were heard outside. The door opened, and the King appeared on the threshold. Like the Marquise he was in a dressing-gown, displaying through the easy folds his well-built figure. A certain sultriness lay over his still handsome face

and a slight flabbiness of the features betrayed the voluptu-
ous habits of their owner's life. On seeing the Prince he
stopped in affronted surprise, obviously unused to finding
another visitor before him in this place and at this hour.
Had the Marquise intended this meeting when she received
her former lover? Was she taking advantage of the only
opportunity she saw open to her of fulfilling the priest's
wish? She was playing a dangerous game if this was the
case.

For a few moments all three stood as if paralyzed. Then
the Marquise fluttered to the King and grasping his hand,
pressed it tenderly to her heart.

"Sire," she said in an ever so tremulous voice, "please
forgive the presence of the Prince de Beauvau. He has come
in great distress to ask a favor of you. I beg you most earn-
estly to be gracious enough to listen to him!"

The King's face betrayed painful embarrassment. "How
could I refuse anything to such a charming petitioner?" he
said hesitantly. "So say what you want of me," he continued, turning slightly to the Prince. His voice was
halting.

The much-desired audience had come to him, but the
Prince seemed unable to grasp the fact. Had the encounter
been too sudden for him? Was it too different in character
from what he had expected? He felt his aversion to the
intercession of the Marquise grow overpowering. There
could be no doubt whatsoever that the King knew of his
previous relations with Reinette. In fact, he came to the
shattering conviction that this knowledge was actually be-

hind the mystery of his successes; that it was the very reason for his unceasing rise to power. In short, that this rise was the compensation, so to speak, which it pleased the King to grant him for the loss of his beloved.

And once more everything became overshadowed by Aigues-Mortes.

The King was patiently waiting for an answer, and the Marquise was visibly trembling in every limb. "Sire," she gasped in a faltering voice, "allow me, I beseech you, to intercede for the Prince. It concerns an error which you in your mercy will surely forgive. The Prince was in Aigues-Mortes, and he released the Huguenot prisoners there. He begs of your great kind heart the royal letter of authority which he should have obtained first."

Saying this she raised both hands in exquisite pleading. The light negligée fell from her beautiful arms, and as she stood in this graceful posture the Prince was once more reminded of a shimmering reptile rearing its head high and performing a seductive dance in the moonlight.

At the words of the Marquise the King raised his finely arched but somewhat too bushy eyebrows so that they darkened his wide forehead like threatening storm-clouds. "I know that, I know that already," he said. "The Prince's chaplain reported the events in Aigues-Mortes to the Archbishop of Paris, as was his duty. You will have to stand your trial for this, Prince, because your action was illegal in every respect. I regret that I can give you no better advice than to leave France as quickly as possible. I shall see to it that you reach the frontier unhindered. Meanwhile the prisoners whom you have released can be rounded up again, and once this is done the matter will be quickly forgotten. Then, after a few months, you can come back to Paris. And now, do not thank me—thank Madame la Marquise."

The final invitation struck the Prince as an expression of the secret triumph which the King was conscious of having gained over him. Again he was silent. Had he failed to understand the King's words, those words which had suddenly relieved him of all anxiety, assured his safety, and banished the fearful spectre of imprisonment from his mind? He was to evade the coming trial by fleeing abroad, and return within measurable time, when everything would be as before: he would be in and out of the Court, success and splendor would continue to accompany his way, he would take part in the receptions of the great, sit at the gaming-tables in the evening, join in the solemn measure of the courtly gavottes; enjoy all the advantages of his high rank and position. In short, the whole brilliant pageant of his life would begin anew. He had only to stretch out his hands and take it up again.

But he could not stretch them out. Quite clearly he heard a faint weak voice which whispered close beside his ear the unforgettable word *"Résistez!"* At that moment he knew that there was no power on earth which could force him to shut his ears to that word. It would pursue him for the rest of his life and confront him again and again whenever there was the temptation to surrender the highest good to personal comfort.

And now in his immediate circumstances something extraordinary happened. His horror of the threatened imprisonment suddenly changed into a horror of the pardon that the King was offering him. He was aware, to his own astonishment, that he had already crossed the frontier which separated him from his former world, and that his former world had finally disappeared before his eyes like a ship in full rigging sinking beneath the waves. An inexorable break with his entire past had taken place, a break against which he had defended himself desperately and which nevertheless he had to acknowledge now. Never, no never, could he deliver up again those prisoners to whom he had given their freedom. This freedom was his own.

The face of the King, who was waiting for an answer, took on an expression of acute impatience. A mask was threatening to fall from it. "Why do you not thank Madame la Marquise?" he asked brusquely. "Do you not consent, perhaps?" The last words were a challenge, and almost hostile.

"No. I do no consent, Sire," the Prince heard himself say. It was as though his power of speech, acting independently of him, had formed his statement out of his own deep inner urge, and without the least effort on the part of the speaker. "No. I do not consent to being pardoned unless the prisoners are also pardoned."

Again the King controlled himself with difficulty. " 'I do not consent!' What do you mean by using such words to me? You know as well as I do that the Edict of Nantes has been revoked."

"But the laws of humanity and mercy have not been revoked."

Once more the Prince heard himself speaking without, as it were, any effort on his own part.

The raised eyebrows of the King were more closely knit together, forming an almost horizontal line across his forehead. The threatening storm was thundering loudly now.

"Do not forget, Prince, that you are speaking to the Most Christian King of France, whose duty it is to guard the faith of this country." He spoke now as a monarch with biting arrogance. "Who will guarantee me that your released prisoners will not endanger that faith?"

"I will, Sire," the Prince, or rather, that new, independent voice which he recognized again and again as his own, replied.

But the King's voice too had now taken on something of an involuntary violence. "How do you propose to assure this guarantee?" he asked. "Will you perchance take your prisoners' place in the Tower of Aigues-Mortes?"

For the third time this day the spectre of the Tower of Aigues-Mortes emerged as a personal threat before the inner eye of the Prince. Did his breakout into spiritual freedom entail physical imprisonment?

There was an embarrassed silence, then the Prince said in a low voice, but very distinctly, "Do not forget, Sire, that there is a freedom against which even the power of the Kings of France is helpless."

The King's voice lowered menacingly. "I believe, Prince,

that it will be best for you if we end this interview," he said. This was an unmistakable order to withdraw.

Yet the Prince did not go. He did not stir from the spot. "Sire, I beg you for an amnesty for the prisoners," he persisted.

Suddenly the King seemed almost to forget his royal dignity. "Can you not see that Madame la Marquise and I wish to be alone?" he demanded imperiously. "What more is it that you want of me?"

And now a factor quite other than the fate of the prisoners entered the lists.

The Prince stood rigidly tense; his anger flamed up! "I should have liked, Sire, to appear before you in mourning attire as the Marquis of Montespan once did before your predecessor."

The King turned white. Then his stricken pride recoiled and struck back. "Do you also remember how long Monsieur de Montespan spent in the Bastille after he had done so?" he asked icily. "No. You don't remember that? Well, you shall have an opportunity of thinking about it."

Then, turning to the Marquise, he said, "I have heard, Madame, that you have been refused Absolution unless you leave Versailles. I shall place no obstacle in the way of your returning to someone who believes he has a right to you." Then, without deigning to say a word of farewell either to the Prince or to the Marquise, he left the room.

When the door had closed behind him the Marquise sank down on an armchair and covered her face with her small energetic hands, which were now so helpless. "It is all over!" she murmured. "This is the end! Oh, why did you speak of Monsieur de Montespan?"

"I should have spoken of him years ago, Reinette," said the Prince. "I should have helped you to defend our love. But I did not help you. I had a part in the base barter. Can you forgive me?"

Involuntarily he slipped into the familiar *"Tu"* of former days. She took no notice, however, but continued her lament: "Ah, that wretched journey to Aigues-Mortes. As soon as you came back I felt the change! What actually happened to you there?"

"This happened, Reinette," he replied. "I met down there a person who sacrifices everything and endures everything for the truth of her life, whereas we have sacrificed the truth of our lives for material success and luxury. But this is over for ever! Do you not also feel liberated?"

"Liberated?" she cried. "Liberated, indeed! Did you not understand, then, what the King meant when he mentioned the Bastille?"

"Oh, yes," he replied gravely. "Yes, I did understand." And as he said it he became aware, to his own astonishment, that all his terror of imprisonment had vanished.

She looked at him with wide uncomprehending eyes. "The King will not spare you," she lamented. "I know him. He has always hated you because he knows what there has been between you and me. Ah, everything he granted me for you was due to this hatred; to the constant feeling that he must compensate you for me. He is too proud to take me from another without paying for it. Now that he has dismissed me, he will no longer feel obliged to have any consideration for you. You must get away! You must do so this very minute if you are to reach the frontier in time!"

"Yes, I shall leave for Aigues-Mortes this very day," he replied calmly.

"For Aigues-Mortes?" she cried, horrified. "You will go to Aigues-Mortes? Do you not understand that by doing so you will lose the last precious bit of time you have?"

She looked at him in speechless astonishment. Then her expression changed. An hour ago this change would have intoxicated the Prince, but the world had changed for him in the interval. Suddenly she threw herself into his arms. "Don't leave me!" she pleaded. "Really, in my heart, it is you alone whom I have always loved!"

He disengaged himself gently from her arms. "Reinette," he said, "I cannot take you with me to the place where I am going. I can only forgive you, and you must forgive me!"

*

We are now nearing the end of this story; its outcome is one which we can only speak of with reserve because the chain of events has been interpreted in various ways, not to say distorted.

The Prince's journey was like a flight. He took an insignificant-looking epiquage; he went without servants; he traveled only by night.

As on his first visit there, it was morning as he approached the notorious Tower of Aigues-Mortes. It reared up more gloomily and repellantly than even before over the melancholy landscape. But this time the Prince felt a silent sympathy with its sad austerity. He felt a deep community of spirit with it. He was ready to identify himself with it and all that it stood for, so ready, indeed, that the sight of it was almost a secret joy.

As he stepped on to the bridge which led over the stagnant moat to the entrance to the Tower he saw a covered country cart at the other side. The commandant of the tower was standing beside the driver, obviously giving him some instructions. When he caught sight of the Prince he left the other man and hurried up to him.

"Thank God you've come in time with the royal mandate," he cried. "I am just releasing Marie Durand as the last of our prisoners. I had kept her back all this time in order to fulfill the formalities. I mean . . . so that I could say I had not acted without the royal consent."

The Prince greeted the commandant but did not refer to the expected royal letter of authority. Instead he asked to be taken to Marie Durand.

They went up to the cart and the commandant signed to the driver to push back the hood. "I had the cart covered over as she can't bear the sunlight," he explained. "All the released women were almost blind from their many years of imprisonment in the semi-darkness of the Tower."

Marie Durand was leaning back, half sitting, half lying in the cart, which had been spread with straw in an effort to make it somewhat comfortable. Her eyes were closed, and she seemed utterly exhausted and listless, as though the strength which had carried her to the end of her long trial had not sufficed to bring her through it.

"Marie Durand," said the commandant, "here is the Prince de Beauvau to see you. Don't you remember? He came here some time ago, not as the fellow-prisoner you took him for at first, but as your liberator."

She made no answer. Now that all the torture was over she was obviously overwhelmed by the whole tragedy of her murdered life. With an almost hostile movement she turned away.

"She heard in the meantime that you're a Catholic," said the commandant apologetically.

The Prince felt inclined to reply, "Really, you know I'm not a Catholic at all. I'm a freethinker," but his lips would not form the words. He was overwhelmed at that moment with irresistible force by the certain reality of God.

"Yes, Marie Durand," he said with trembling lips, trying hard to hide his shattering emotion, "I am a Catholic and as such I share the responsibility for your fate. But can you not shake hands with me all the same?"

She remained silent. It was plain that she was utterly broken. Then the Prince saw the blind eyes opening. Her hand felt its way towards his head. "God bless you, Prince," she said simply. And the cart started to move.

When it had disappeared the Prince turned to the young commandant and said, slowly and sadly: "And now, my friend, conduct me into your tower as prisoner."

The commandant looked at him uncomprehendingly, but the Prince continued calmly, "You see, I have not brought you the royal letter of authority for the release of the prisoners which you rightly expected. The King has not approved their release. It rests only upon my independent command, which was illegal."

The young commandant turned white. "Then I am lost," he said tonelessly.

"I believe," replied the Prince, "that you can save yourself if you take me prisoner. You will be acting entirely correctly if you do so. Therefore I ask you to do it. Lock me into the Tower in place of the prisoners. No, don't hesitate," he continued. "I'm bound to be imprisoned in any case, and perhaps it is particularly right and significant that it be here."

*

The chonicler cannot vouch for the truth of what has yet to be told. In Aigues-Mortes itself—that is to say, in the little hamlet of the name—a legend persisted for a long time to the effect that the authorities had wanted to keep Marie Durand back as the last of the prisoners, but that the Prince de Beauvau had offered to take her place in prison as guarantor for her, and this version of the story does in fact correspond to a wider view of things. One thing is certain, however, that the Prince de Beauvau became an inmate of the Tower of the Constant at his own wish, though for how long we do not know. Was this tower the mysterious prison which actually meant spiritual freedom for him, that spiritual freedom to which Marie Durand had borne witness before him? Did he wish to convince himself of the reality of that freedom, or was the desire to make atonement the determining motive? We do not know. Only the letter of the Marquise, which brought this imprisonment to an end, has been preserved to us. It contains the following lines:

"The King has consented to pardon you unconditionally, Prince; and I do not think that he will insist on the prisoners being rounded up again, either. The order to this effect has been sent to the commandant. I have wrung it from the King. To save you I have had to remain what I have been to the King for many years now—the mistress whom he cast aside in a moment of anger but soon longed for most ardently again. In the night of love which I gave him on returning to him, the decision in your favor was made. Farewell. We shall never meet again. Reinette has resigned herself for ever to that fate which separates us! For me there is no reprieve but the consciousness that by my final fall I have served you. My punishment is at the same time my Absolution, the only Absolution to which I still have any right. For now I have really done for love of you what I once strove for out of ambition. Now, though separated forever from you, I am,

Ever yours,
Reinette."

*

Actually, the proceedings which had been initiated against the Prince were silenced; nor was there another word about rearresting the prisoners of Aigues-Mortes who had been released. We know that Marie Durand and her companions were allowed to spend the last years of their lives in their modest homes. The Prince returned to his governorship and devoted himself to the duties of his office. He was never seen at Court again either in Paris or in Versailles. For years there were recurrent rumors that he had secretly become a Protestant; this was probably because he exerted himself unremittingly to better the lot of the persecuted Huguenots. Pére Laroche, the only person who could probably have denied or confirmed these reports correctly, for it is known that he visited the Prince several times, had to leave the country with his fellow Jesuits shortly after the Prince's release and was never heard of again. So there is an impenetrable silence which surrounds the Prince on every side. The remainder of his life passed almost as quietly and insignificantly as that of Marie Durand. To be sure, he publicly professed himself a member of the Catholic Church but no one really believed him to be a Catholic in truth, the more so since the freethinkers continued zealously to claim him as one of their number. He did not deem these rumors worth contradicting, but after his death a prayer, written in his own hand, was found among his papers. Its tattered condition betrayed much use. It read:

My God, in Thine unsearchable councils, Thou hast permitted those to whom Thou hast entrusted the faith of their fathers in this country, to lend themselves to the perse-

*cution of those who, in a time of atheistic delusion con-
fessed, though in a form strange to us, to the rejected faith
in Thee. Thou gavest them the strength to persevere in that
faith at the sacrifice of their freedom and often even their
lives. In a time of unscrupulous seeking for comfort and
success Thou gavest them the spirit of sacrifice, and the
grace to sing Thy praises in wretched prisons and chained
to the galleys. Thou didst grant them the inestimable
privilege of bearing testimony to the Passion of Christ in
their own sufferings. It hath pleased Thee, my God, to
permit them to empty the last drop of the chalice of suffering
and thereby awaken my heart, which had turned away from
Thee. Permit this heart to intercede now for its rescuers.
Grant me the grace to profess in the Church of my fathers
the faith in Thee which they have given back to this heart
of mine. Permit me, precisely as a member of this Church,
to show love and respect for the persecuted and to demon-
strate to the end of my life that we, the children of the old
Faith, are also children of mercy. Help me to endure with
patience, in reparation for the irreparable guilt of the per-
secutors, that my orthodoxy is called in question. On behalf
of my brethren in the Faith who have not yet been given
the grace of repentance, I repent of this guilt. And I commend to Thine immeasurable love the final reunion and
reconciliation of all separated Christians, Amen.*

THE JUDGEMENT OF
THE SEA

THE JUDGEMENT OF THE SEA

WHEN the royal ships were sailing across the channel to Cornwall, the raging storm against which they had been struggling in the beginning was smothered with fantastic suddenness by a soundless calm, whereupon the little Prince was taken ill with a most extraordinary malady, the like of which had never before been observed in a child of such tender years. While the sea seemed to sink deeper and deeper into the drowsy intoxication of a leaden slumber, the poor little child was seized with absolute sleeplessness. In vain did his young wet-nurse sing him the usual lullabies, in vain did she offer him her breast, on which he normally fell asleep contented; he refused all nourishment, craving only for the sweet milk of slumber which no one could give him. And while the wide open eyes in his pale solemn face grew larger and larger, his little body wasted away as if consumed by the hunger of those over-large, over-watchful eyes, which would not close for a single moment.

The physicians on board the royal ship were at a loss;

they could give no counsel. The coasts of Normandy, from which the ships had sailed, seemed as hopelessly out of reach as those of Cornwall, towards which they were trying to sail, for not the faintest breath of wind touched the limp sails.

Finally, seeing that the child's condition was becoming more and more disquieting, those who were with the royal parents took courage to remind them that the hostage Anne de Vitré was aboard one of the escort ships, and that her countryman Budoc asserted she was one of those who could still sing the Old Breton slumber song.

King John was alarmed at this suggestion; he feared to have Anne de Vitré called, for he thought of his last raid on the Bretons, of their burned towns and trampled fields. But most of all he thought of the young Duke, the gentle boy whom he had carried away in that raid and murdered with his own hand at Rouen. And so he replied that he had known long since that the Bretons were still heathen magicians but he himself was a good Christian and did not wish to have anything to do with their evil cradle songs. Had they forgotten Anne's grandmother, the woman called Avoise, who had gone through the Castle of Reaux by night singing as the English troops lay in their beds there? Not a single man of them had risen the next morning.

So the little Prince continued to suffer, his over-large, over-watchful eyes wide open while the sea continued to sleep undisturbed. But after a few days, when King John had fled to the Senechal's ship to escape from the sleepless eyes of his child, the Queen, in desperation, sent for Budoc and ordered him to row one of her serving women over to the Breton woman under cover of darkness.

Anne de Vitré had not yet lain down to rest, but was sitting on the deck of her ship under the starry tent of heaven, and questioning the sea, as her people were wont to do when they knew of no other counsel. It gave Anne a deep calm confidence to know that she could turn to the sea; it gave her a feeling of assurance such as her heart had not known for a long time. In Rouen she had always felt so helpless; there everything had seemed frightening and uncertain to her, but on the sea she felt secure. On the land there were woods and caves, and dark castles with dreadful dungeons; places where evil secrets can easily hide —but on the sea all things reveal themselves as they are. Anne thought of the times when men were tried for their lives in her country, of how the people entrusted themselves to the sea and submitted to its judgment, and how the sea recognized the guilty and kept them in its clutches, but set the innocent on land. And it never erred in its judgment. After all, the sea was not like finite, short-sighted man; the sea was God's greatest and most powerful creature, it came nearest to Himself in omnipotence, it was very close to His heaven—it was almost like God. You had to ask the sea if you hoped to hear the voice of God, and what voice could Anne de Vitré still hope to hear but His?

All the people around her shrank back timidly and wrapped themselves in impenetrable silence whenever she tried to find out about the young Duke of her country; it was as though his name had been completely wiped from their memories. And after all Anne de Vitré had a right to ask about him since it was for her young Duke's sake that she had been delivered up to this foreign king: she was held hostage for the oath of allegiance which had been wrung from the Duke. It was for him that she had had to leave her devoted parents and her loving brothers and sisters, and all the beauties of her sorrowful country. If she had not left her people he would have had to go—but a Duke must not desert his people. This was what her father had impressed upon her when parting from her, and thus Anne repeated his words in her heart again and again each day. Otherwise she would long since have died of grief and loneliness among the Britons. But she had been able to go on living, for if she had gone into a strange land for the sake of the young Duke of her people, he had remained in the homeland for her. If she had to be a prisoner for him, then he had freedom for her: he was at home in her place; he was her freedom. Her real life was not here among this hard alien race; her real life was the life of her young Duke. Surely Anne must have a right to ask about this, her real life! But even though she might get no answer from man, the sea would not refuse her an answer. The sea was just; the sea was almost like God. Anne de Vitré listened.

No sound arose from the motionless water. The ships lay upon it like dead black swans, almost as if they had been frozen on to it. Never in her life had Anne seen the sea so calm. One would really have thought that it was sleeping. But the sea did not sleep, as these Britons thought it did; it was only silent, as God too is only silent when He seems to be sleeping. And when God has been silent for a long time He will speak. Anne de Vitré listened once more.

Suddenly she seemed to hear a faint sound like the beat of a wave close by the bow of the ship; it was as though the sea were about to open its mouth. And as Anne rose to her feet—for it is but seemly to listen to the answer of the sea standing—she saw the dark outlines of a man rise up above the water like a creature of the deep. She heard a short, subdued cry such as the seafarers of her country use when their boat is putting in somewhere. And now Anne de Vitré could see the boat silently gliding towards the ship. She recognized the man in it. It was Budoc.

Anne was disappointed, for Budoc would only disturb her as she questioned the sea—Budoc was a turncoat and a traitor. He had long ago forgotten that, like herself, he was here among the Britons as a hostage for the young Duke of their people. Budoc dwelt among the Britons as if he were one of them. Anne despised and avoided him although he had once been a close friend and a guest in her father's house. Yet sometimes when their eyes met unexpectedly, she was overcome with homesickness as if she saw her distant country before her. But that must surely be an illusion.

Meanwhile Budoc had tied his boat to the ship and helped the serving woman on board. Anne could not imagine why the Queen should send for her at such a late hour, but she was too proud to ask because she would of course have had to use Budoc's help as the serving woman did when delivering her message—the woman did not understand the Breton language, and Anne did not understand the hated Briton tongue. She had never tried to learn it; but of course Budoc had learned it!

Anne followed them in silence. But now, as she sat opposite Budoc in the little boat, close above the water, very near to the deep, clear, omniscient eye of the sea, it suddenly seemed to her that he was beginning a mysterious conversation with her in the darkness, not with the voice of his mouth but with the voice of his blood, that ancient Celtic blood which flowed in the veins of both of them, deep as the beautiful springs of their country and dark as the woods of the sorcerers, and wild as the wave-lashed rocky coasts where the "Woman of Death" croons the slumber song of their mothers in the ears of drowning sea-farers. Although it was too dark to see Budoc's eyes she seemed to see through them, into the abyss of an unshakable fidelity; not the tender, noble fidelity of her own love, but the fidelity of hatred, the daringly cunning fidelity which does not shrink from playing the turncoat to the enemy in order the more surely to betray him. Anne felt that the same pain was quivering through both of them; and she felt that at any moment she would have to listen to the voice of his mouth speaking of the young Duke who was the lord of them both. No, Budoc would not dare speak before the serving woman; it was so alarmingly silent out here on the sea that even the softest whisper would resound to the horizon.

Only when the small boat, rocking slightly, lay close by

the bow of the royal ship and the serving woman had already climbed aboard, Budoc brought his dark face close to hers and whispered in her ear, "The Duke is dead. The King himself was his murderer. The sea has judged him, and you . . . you . . . you. . . ." It was as though a wild feeling of triumph robbed him of speech. He raised her up in his naked arms—for a moment she did not know whether he was going to fling her up in the air like a jubilant shout of revenge, or cast her into the sea. But no, he had already set her down on the deck.

Bewildered and dazed, Anne entered the pavilion of the royal ship. The interior was in semi-darkness; only from the entrance, where the sailcloth was turned back and bound to two carved pillars, a glimmer of the sea was visible, white as the stars.

The young Queen was standing there, straight and graceful, but her little insignificant face under the golden winged cap was tear-stained. She addressed Anne in hurried, timid words. She spoke so anxiously one might have surmised that she, as Anne, was thinking of the murdered young Duke, but she was thinking only of her small sick child. Anne did not understand her, Budoc's words were still ringing like a peal of bells in her ears; the frail boyish shade of the murdered Duke seemed to absorb all her attention. She did not even realize that the Queen was speaking to her—she took no notice of her. But then she heard Budoc's voice again. "Anne de Vitré," he said, "Madame the Queen wants to know whether you would be able to sing the Breton slumber song to her sick child?"

Anne understood Budoc just as little as she had understood the young Queen. It was as if he spoke to her in the language of these strangers, and she made no answer.

The arched eyebrows of the young Queen moved a little, as if they wished to threaten Anne. But then her little insignificant face became quite helpless again. She tore off the golden chain from her neck and laid it over Anne; she stripped off her bracelets and offered them to her; she kissed Anne on both cheeks. Anne felt the weight of the chains and the bangles on her body; she perceived the wetness of tears on her face, but still she did not understand. All this while Budoc stood there, quietly waiting. His dark face, detached and impassive.

Now the Queen turned to him again. "Ah, Budoc," she sobbed, "I believe Anne has forgotten the song. Do please ask her to remember it. Beg her to; you see she doesn't understand my words."

"Anne de Vitré," said Budoc, "Madame the Queen is afraid that you have forgotten the song, but I know that you have not. You were already old enough when you heard your mother sing it by the cradle of your little brother Alain—the little Alain who drowned in the sea afterwards. I remember you exactly in those days: you used to lie in the lower part of the old trunk-bed singing with her, singing like a little bird in its nest until you fell asleep."

Anne remained silent although she now understood Budoc; her eyes filled with tears. How could Budoc ever think that she would sing to the child of the royal murderer the cradle song, the sweet cradle song which her mother had sung to her little brother Alain? Was Budoc a traitor after all? Her child-like face became quite stern and pitiless. The young Queen looked at her with dismay; like a poor woman of the people begging an alms. "Oh, God, she will not sing to my child!" she wailed. "She will not do it! Ah, Budoc, do please speak to her again! Persuade her, tell her she must have mercy on us!"

"Anne," said Budoc, "you understand now what the Queen means, but you don't understand what I mean. You will not sing the cradle song to the child because he is the child of the royal murderer. But you can sing it to him, and for that very reason! Just think once more of your little brother Alain—little Alain who was drowned in the sea afterwards. To all who are drowned in the sea the "Woman of Death" sings the song which she has heard their mothers sing by their cradles. It is the same song, Anne, exactly the same song. Your grandmother Avoise knew it, and you know it too: the child to whom the beginning is sung falls asleep, and the child to whom it is sung to the end never wakes again. You must sing it to the end for the child of Madame the Queen! You know the beginning—the beginning and the end—cradle and wave are one. Now do you understand at last that you . . . you . . . you. . . ."

Once more the note of jubilation, which choked his words, had come into his voice. But now Anne understood: the sea had answered, the sea had passed judgement, the sea demanded this child. Truly the sea was just; the sea was almost like God. She remained quite still for a moment like one praying; then, slowly, she removed the Queen's chains and bangles from her neck and arms, walked up to the breast-rail of the ship, and threw them into the sea. Her face was as white and impassive as the sea. She did not look at the Queen. She kept her eyes turned only towards the sea. "I will sing the cradle song," she said.

But now the young Queen became uneasy. "Budoc, why has she taken off my jewelry?" she asked, tremulously. "Chains are fetters—I wanted to bind her to me with my chains. Why did she give them to the sea? Does she seek an alliance with it?"

Budoc replied lightly that he thought custom required it of those about to sing the Breton slumber song. But the young Queen was not reassured. "So she is in league with the sea when she sings!" she cried, beside herself. "But the sea is our enemy! The sea is cruel! It is holding my little sick child fast and preventing us from bringing him to land! What kind of a covenant is it that she has with the sea?" And she looked searchingly into the eyes of Anne de Vitré.

Anne had now turned back from the breast-rail of the ship and was standing in the dimly lit opening of the tent. The whitish radiance of the motionless water outlined her figure from behind as if with a silver pencil; it was still as slender and as touchingly unrounded as that of the young girl who had been delivered up a hostage to the Britons a year and a day before. It was as though Anne had not yet blossomed fully into womanhood although she was already in her first tender maturity. But after all, Anne could not flower in a strange land; her life was as a motionless shadow.

The Queen's eyes in that small face of hers, suddenly took on an odd visionary expression: it seemed to her as though she were really seeing Anne de Vitré for the first time at this moment.

Budoc had motioned the ladies and serving women to leave the pavilion and to escort their mistress from it if Anne began to sing. But the young Queen hesitated. "No, no!" she protested. "I will not go out. I will remain here while Anne is singing. I will not leave my child alone with her if she has a pact with the sea!" She sounded very much afraid of Anne de Vitré.

The women tried to smile reassuringly. The eldest of them, a kinswoman of the royal house, went to encourage the young Queen: Anne was only going to do what had urgently been requested of her; now they must trust her and act as Breton custom prescribed. Anyway, they would have to leave the pavilion if they did not want to be put to sleep themselves.

At the word "trust" the young Queen suddenly began to tremble. The little silver discs with which the edges of her golden bonnet were decorated began to whisper and flutter like the leaves of an aspen. She stared into Anne's lonely young face as if her eyes were feeling their way through its sorrowful loveliness to the countenance of a Medusa within. "But I cannot trust her!" she cried. "Just look at her! We have never really looked at her before!"

Once more the women tried to smile reassuringly. The aged cousin of the royal house renewed her persuasions. Anne held so tender and innocent an expression, why would the royal cousin not trust her child to her? After all Anne herself was hardly more than a child!

"But that's just it! That's just it!" stammered the Queen. "Do you not understand? Of course she doesn't understand what a little child is. She has neither husband nor child. She has no life at all, and she doesn't even desire one. She has given away her life to someone else . . . to someone who is no longer alive." The last words came like a mere breath from her lips. No one understood what they meant.

Now the Queen became completely beside herself. "But you must understand me," she cried. "You must! We know, don't we, that the Bretons can kill people with their slumber song—have you forgotten about the British soldiers in the Château of Reaux?"

At these words the courtly aristocratic faces of the women suddenly forgot their smiles. The aged relative made a motherly movement: how could the royal cousin speak so? We must not offend Anne de Vitré like that! Kill a child? No one would have the heart to do that!

The young Queen, barely whispering, continued: "Oh, yes, indeed, yes indeed, people do find it in their hearts to kill children," she breathed. "These days people find it in their hearts to do anything—anything at all. You know as well as I do . . . the whole court knows it . . . everyone in

Rouen knew it . . . don't keep on pretending! Oh, God, I cannot say it! Why do you question me?"

The women had turned pale under their paint and powder. Did Madame the Queen perchance mean the young Duke of the Bretons? He was still a boy, almost a child. They did not dare to look at each other, for no one of them knew how much the other knew, so efficiently had every rumor of the crime been silenced.

For a few moments it was as though even the sea outside were holding its breath. Suddenly the ladies began to feel uneasy; their smooth suave courtiers' faces assumed an expression of helplessness; they turned around timidly as if they feared someone might be listening outside the pavilion. Only the good simple eyes of the royal cousin looked guilelessly unembarrassed, for the old generation cannot imagine the horrors of modern times. What did the Queen think they had been asking her about, she inquired placatingly? None of the women had uttered a single question; neither had Budoc nor Anne, and there was nobody else there. The Queen was making a mistake.

"But someone keeps questioning me all the time," murmured the Queen. "Do you not notice it? It's as if we were on trial here, being cross-examined before a court. And before a court one must confess if one wants to obtain mercy. But I have nothing to confess. I don't know why my little baby cannot sleep, and I don't want to be asked about it any more. It is a terrible thing when little children cannot sleep any more—only criminals are sleepless! But my little child has committed no crime. There must be some mistake. Why should he suffer? Budoc, tell Anne there's been a mistake. She needn't sing—I'll do it myself!"

"Anne," began Budoc, "it seems that the sea is demanding the confession of Madame the Queen before it can carry out its sentence. But she cannot bring her lips to utter it. Don't be annoyed, you will have to wait a little longer."

Anne had been standing there the whole time, completely lost in her own thoughts, intent upon recalling the song which she was to sing. It was such a long time since she had heard it; she had to summon up all her powers to remember it; she dared not take any notice of what was happening around her. At Budoc's words she looked up for the first time. An expression of astonishment came into her impassive face. Where now was the graceful Queen who had held such gay court in Rouen at the time when that great impenetrable silence had arisen concerning the young Duke of the Bretons? Where now was the painted, bejewelled woman who had always smilingly evaded Anne's trembling questions about him? Where was the flatterer who had pretended to be so nice to her, even here on the ship? Now, all of a sudden, there was only a little wild desperate face, mirror-clear as the naked stones of the strand washed by the sea. Yes, truly, on the sea everything is revealed.

Anne did not venture to speak a word. She nodded to Budoc signifying that she would wait. How could she refuse to do so? The sea was waiting too; the sea was in no hurry; it had the breath of eternity; it was almost like God. No one could escape God and eternity.

A soft breath of wind came from outside—the waters must have begun to stir. It was as though the sea were mounting its judgement seat. To Anne de Vitré it seemed suddenly strangely bright for the middle of the night.

Meanwhile the Queen herself had sat down beside the cradle and begun to sing in her small thin voice. As she sang the melody became confused, the words became senselessly jumbled and she sang the wrong notes. It was as though the little song which she had started were going quite mad in her mouth. Suddenly she stopped and said in a faint, gasping voice: "My God! What's this? It's getting so bright, and the little Prince must sleep! The tent will have to be closed."

Her eyes fell on Anne, who was still standing in the entrance, now no longer as if drawn with a soft silver pencil but rather as if enveloped in radiance from a star: the sea behind her had begun to shine. At sight of her the Queen uttered a cry and threw herself over the cradle as if to protect the child with her body.

"Why is she still there? Why is she still there?" she sobbed. "Have I not said to tell her that the little one will be able to go to sleep himself? Yes, I believe he's already asleep—just look . . . look. . . ."

With a trembling hand she raised the curtains of the cradle.

Suddenly it had become so clear it seemed as though the brightness of the sea had come on board and were sweeping into the middle of the pavilion. One could see every corner of that tented space; and one could recognize in the half-light of the open cradle the solemn face of the little Prince. The young wet-nurse suddenly began sobbing loudly and could not be consoled. The Queen's ladies were crying too, but the Queen herself sat there as if turned into a pillar of salt with her tearless eyes staring into the wide open eyes of her child.

At last the aged relative touched the Queen on the shoulder and said compassionately: "Dearest cousin, Anne de Vitré is still here, will you not open your heart and have confidence in her? For it's not just by mischance that the little Prince cannot sleep."

The Queen made no answer but began murmuring in a low voice. No one could say to whom she was speaking—it was as though she were rendering an account to an invisible father-confessor. "No, it is not by a mischance that the little Prince cannot sleep," she whispered, "and I know why it is not. It is because there is nothing on earth more frightful than to murder a child—and we have murdered a child. When you are silent in the face of a crime, you give your consent to it. And I have kept silent about it—every one of us has done so—the whole Court has done so. We have kept silent, and our silence has cried to heaven. We have eaten and drunk, we have dressed ourselves up and adorned ourselves as if nothing had happened; we have laughed and danced. And yes, we have even slept soundly although one would have thought that no one could have slept any more at Rouen. But we could . . . we did. Why should we not have slept? There was no judge who could have wakened us, for the judges were also asleep. Of course they had to sleep—they were ordered to do so. Only my little child can no longer sleep!" And she looked around her with the air of someone who had completely forgotten where she was.

The women had slipped out of the tent one after another. Even the Queen's cousin had withdrawn, perplexed. Only Anne de Vitré was still there, and in the background, Budoc. His face seemed the only dark thing left in the lightfilled room. The Queen took no notice of him; she leaned back her head again as if she would cry out in sheer anguish. As she did so her golden winged cap slipped back on to her neck, and her golden hair came loose and fell into her face like a lion's mane. She stood up and walked a few steps toward Anne. It seemed as though she wished to throw herself on her knees at Anne's feet, but that her whole being clamored in its depths to struggle with the girl. Her small, doll-like face, so pitiable without color or adornment, was wiped out, completely overwhelmed and blotted out by its own prototype. She was now no longer herself. She was only a part of the vast elemental forces from the nameless mother's womb of Nature.

"Anne," she cried, "I know that you are in league with the sea which you Bretons say is just, and almost like God. I submit myself to its judgement. But a person is surely at liberty to plead for mercy before every judge. And so I plead: Kill me but save my child! I swear that I will surrender myself to you when we land in Cornwall. Sing there if you like, and where you like. I will give you the key to Bristol Castle. You may go through all the passages there in the night as your grandmother did through the Castle of Reaux when the British garrison lay there in their beds. And when I hear your voice outside my room I myself will open the door to your song and listen to it willingly until I can no longer hear. No, do not fear that I will flee from you! Ah, Anne, you have no child! You cannot understand me—but you must believe me, it is not difficult to die for this little child. I know it—once before, I nearly died for him—the time I brought him into this world. Ah, Anne, believe me! I pray you, believe me!"

She had quite forgotten that the Breton girl could not understand her language.

Anne felt vaguely that the other woman was struggling with her for the life of her child. Once more her noble young face took on an unyielding expression and she shut her eyes to the Queen. She was concentrating completely on the song which she seemed to hear from afar, from the beautiful springs of her homeland and the woods of the sorcerer Merlin, and the sea-lashed rocky coasts where the "Woman of Death" crooned the cradle song of their mothers into the ears of drowning fishermen. And now Anne walked into the great twilight chamber of the Castle of Reaux, softly, as her long dead ancestress had once walked there; no, as the "Woman of Death" had entered when she came to listen by Alain's cradle. Anne heard her singing the sweet lullaby of her mother—and her heart began to beat faster. It seemed to her as if she were reawakening with terrible suddenness to her own, her real life. And now she would see Alain again too—her resolute young face became undescribably tender at the thought.

The Queen never took her eyes off her. Suddenly something like a breath of relief passed through her whole body. She grasped Anne by the hands and drew her over to the cradle. Anne felt a sisterly kiss on her lips and heard the fading rustle of a dress. For a few seconds she remained like a sleeper who resists wakening at the end of a dream. Then she realized that the Queen had left her alone with the child. The hour had come. She did not dare to open her eyes. With her hands folded fervently, looking like the picture of one in prayer, she began to sing.

At first her voice sounded very shy. She sang without words, only humming the notes, murmuring them tenderly, and beginning at the beginning again and again with the first ones, which sounded like little waves breaking on the strand and gently rocking a small boat back and forth. But then the words leaped out from the melody as if of themselves—gracious innocent words in childish rhymes. To Anne it was as though her mother were singing them aloud to her; she did not noice that her own voice had become like her mother's. Since she had been with the British, Anne had never once sung; she no longer knew her own voice; she thought she was listening to her mother's: now she was lying once more in the big trunk-bed in the Château of Reaux and needed only to join in as her mother sang her little brother Alain to sleep.

As soon as Alain fell asleep the mother went out to call

the old maid-servant Enora to come in and sit with the children. Until Enora came Anne was alone with Alain; she could be his little mother for a while. Alain needed that because he was so very tiny. Every time she looked at him she was filled with tender compassion, although he really was a rosy faced healthy child. But something could easily happen to such a tiny child; Ann dared not let him out of her sight; she would have loved to take him in her arms and press him to her heart, but her mother and Enora had forbidden her to do that; Anne herself was still so small she could have let Alain fall.

"But when I'm big, may I take Alain in my arms?" Anne had begged.

"When you're big," Enora had replied, "you'll take a child in your arms—a child to whom you yourself have given life."

It was often a long time before Alain fell asleep and one had to begin singing again and again, tirelessly, just like the little waves on the shore when they rock a little boat.

Anne imagined she perceived the gentle rocking of the cradle which stood beside her on the trunk-bed. By now it should be time to hear the gentle, steady breathing of the sleeper; that soft heavy breathing of a child always filled Anne with such tenderness. She stopped singing and listened, and she became aware that only she had been singing; her mother must have gone out already to call Enora— she was alone with Alain. When she sat up straight in her own half of the high-backed bed, she used to be able to look down into the other half of the bed, right into Alain's face as he lay there in his cradle, sleeping so peacefully, his two sturdy little fists clenched one at each side of his rosy face as if in touching ignorance of his strength. Anne had to smile at the memory—it had always been such a joy to look at him and to know that she was protecting him.

Anne opened her eyes and bent down. There stood the cradle right before her, white as whitethorn. Alain was lying in it, but he was not rosy, and he hadn't his little fists clenched either. Alain—Oh God, it was not Alain at all—it was the little Prince who couldn't sleep and whose life the sea was demanding! Anne stared at him in horror. His tiny face was as white as the flowers on the cradle; his hair was stuck to his forehead wet with fear and perspiration; and the corners of his mouth were drawn down by suffering. But in spite of all this there was something easy and comfortable about his little face; his breathing was barely audible, but gentle and peaceful. He had shut his eyes, he was asleep: Anne had sung him to sleep.

She felt a strange confusion, and suddenly a feeling of tender compassion, the same feeling which used to overwhelm her when she looked at Alain. She forgot completely who this child was, she saw only that he was even tinier and in greater need of protection than her little brother had been: the longer she looked at him the more touching he seemed to her. She would love to take him in her arms as she had always wanted to take Alain. Then why did she not do so? No one could stop her doing so now for of course she was grown up. "When you're big,"

Enora had said, "you'll take a child in your arms, a child to whom you yourself will have given life."

Anne felt a piercing grief, a grief as of being dragged away for a second time from her harsh yet beautiful homeland—no, rather, from the primitive essence of her own deepest being. For was she not standing here to deliver a child up to death? Shuddering with horror she looked at the infant. It would not take long—not as long as it had taken her grandmother Avoise to sing the slumber-song to the Britons who had occupied Château Reaux—for of course the little Prince was so weak and sickly! If Anne sang just a little longer his breathing would become inaudible, and a little longer still and it would begin to fail, and yet a little longer and it would cease, lulled to sleep then washed away by this gentle dreamy melody, which sounded as childish and innocent as those soft waves on the shore as they rock a boat and yet was as near to the abysmal depths as these—yes, as near as sleep is to death—and that is so near that both can be called by the same name.

Now the child suddenly started crying—Alain too would often start crying loudly in that frightened way in the midst of the sweetest slumber—one could have thought that he had seen upon him the eye of the "Woman of Death," who had stood beside his cradle. Involuntarily Anne stepped back a pace. As she did so she became aware that the cover had half slid off the cradle; she came nearer and drew it up carefully. Again the child cried out. Anne had to be careful not to waken him. But there, he had wakened after all: for an instant her gaze was held by the over-large, solemn eyes of the child—it was as though this tiny creature knew the fate awaiting him. Suddenly she thought of the young Duke of her people: he had probably looked at his royal murderer just like that in the last moment of his life. Growing pale, she turned towards the sea—it was as though she wanted to wipe from her sight the picture there in the cradle just as she had removed the Queen's jewels from her body a little time before.

Once more she clasped her hands and began to sing.

Now her voice was even softer than before; it had taken on an ardent and imploring tone, in fact, an almost adjuring note. She seemed to be appealing to the sea to support her, but she could not look at it while she sang; she had to close her eyes once more.

She was back in the half-dark chamber of her parental home, but she no longer heard the sweet singing of her mother. Instead she heard the voice of her grandmother Avoise singing as she had sung in that night to the British soldiers who had taken possession of the Château of Reaux. Anne had been awake at the time although the old nursemaid Enora had stuck wax in her ears. All the family and servants of the Château Reaux had had to do so that night so that they would not fall into that sleep with the Britons. But Anne had loosened the wax a little bit, and every time Dame Avoise had passed by her door on her way through the Château, she had been able to hear her voice for a moment: it was thin and clear like the silver hair on the old lady's head; it seemed incomprehensible that this gentle voice could have overcome all those many, many strong men.

Towards morning Enora had opened the door a little way; in the pale light of the dawn Anne had seen through the narrow opening the naked arms of the men who had slipped behind Dame Avoise, their swords in their hands—to strike down any of the Britons who should stagger up from their sleeping-places—but none did. Those men had a wild sombre joy on their faces as if they were finding it hard to hold back shouts of victory; but there was no jubilation in the face of Dame Avoise. It was quiet, mysterious and open, yet it seemed to Anne much more horrifying than the faces of the men; at that time she did not know why. But now she knew. A woman cannot give herself up to being an instrument of death—woman exists to give life. Anne could feel a yearning rising from the very depths of her being and the remotest sources of her blood, a soft and tender feeling, yet nonetheless strong and powerful and in fact compelling.

Trembling, she shrank farther and farther away from the cradle and towards the opening of the tent; so far that she tasted the salt of the sea on her lips. But the nearer she came to the breast-rail of the ship, the more demanding became her desire. It seemed to her as though the sea were searching through her closed eyes into her innermost being; it became as translucently clear in there as it had been just now under the tent when the Queen had made her confession of guilt—Anne could see into every fold of her heart:

suddenly she could no longer sing. It was as though the sea had drawn her too before its judgment seat. She wanted to fall on her knees and implore its mercy, but she could no longer do even that, so greatly did she fear for the child—she could only escape now into her own mercy, she could only save herself by the cradle.

The child lay in a terrifying quiet. Anne had no choice; she had to take him in her arms to assure herself that he was still alive. As she did her hands trembled: he was light as a new-born infant. Anne had never held a small child in her arms before and she shuddered as she felt the warmth of the tiny body against hers. The infant was breathing, it was sleeping, but more deeply than before. Anne felt as overjoyed as if she herself were recovering from a mortal illness. "It must feel like this," she thought, "to have given birth to a child. It must feel like this!" At the same moment Enora's words came back to her mind, but now a mysterious sweetness mingled with the memory. "I have given him life," she thought, "I have given him life—he's sleeping, he's well again, he's saved." And all at once a deep peace came over her as if she had now fulfilled the meaning of her own life. Again and again she repeated the words, "I have given him life—I have given him life." In her joy she had forgotten everyone and everything else and she felt as if she were all alone in the world with the child.

But she was suddenly aware that this was not so; the thought of Budoc occurred to her. And now she actually saw him emerging from the back of the tent. He spoke no word; but he looked at her as though he had never let her out of his sight the whole time. She tried to ask, "What do you want of me?" but she knew that already. Again she looked into his eyes—through his eyes—into the depths of a fierce unswerving fidelity. These eyes asked her: "Will you sing to the end?"

She shook her head in silence and pressed the child to her breast. Budoc's dark face paled with pain and anger. He stepped up to her, so close that she felt his breath on her face. "Anne," he whispered, "you know that the 'Woman of Death' stands by the cradle of all who drown in the sea—you were still a child when she came to your little brother Alain. Are you really sure that she came for him alone?"

There was a veiled threat in his words. Anne understood it instantly. She looked at his naked arms which had lifted her out of the boat a short while ago when she did not know whether he wanted to throw her up in the air like a jubilant cry of vengeance, or fling her into the sea. But now—curiously—she felt no fear; it seemed to her that Budoc no longer had any power over her. She smiled at him. She no longer believed in the "Woman of Death."

He looked at her fixedly. "Will you sing to the end?" he asked; and she knew within herself he was asking for the last time. Again she shook her head in silence and pressed the babe to her breast. Budoc became yet a shade paler; never would Anne have believed that this swarthy face could turn so terribly white. Slowly he turned to the opening of the tent and let the drawn up sailcloth drop behind him.

Now the two were almost in darkness. Anne could no longer make out Budoc's form, but the nearness of his naked arms seemed terrifying: involuntarily her thoughts went back to the men who had crept along behind Dame Avoise. Like lightning the certainty flashed through her mind: those arms are seeking the child. Uttering a faint cry she pulled back the curtain and with the child pressed to her heart, rushed on to the deck. The next moment she was surrounded by the Queen's ladies.

They took the little prince out of her arms. She heard the young Queen's faint cry of joy at the sight of the sleeping child; she heard the happy excited chorus of whispers. In the rejoicing none of them took any notice of her—after all, it was not her child to whom she had given life, it was the child of the foreign woman, the child of the enemy woman and of the royal murderer. Anne watched them as they laid the babe on the breast of the robust young wet-nurse, who carried it triumphantly back into the tent, followed by all the others. Anne was alone once more under the starry dome of heaven—alone as she had been shortly before, when she had questioned the sea about her young Duke. . . .

But the sea was now questioning her about him! And Anne had to render an account of herself; she had to render an account to this holy, this dread element from which she had fled just now in her mortal anxiety for the child. There it lay, looking as white as if all the stars of the constellations had been drowned in it; as stern as the mirror of an iron law; as motionless and fixed as an all-seeing eye. Once more it seemed to Anne as though a great light was searching through her very being. She did not try to hide. Where should Anne have hidden herself from the sea? The sea was like God! Anne had questioned it, and it had answered her, it had entrusted to her the execution of its judgement—its holy and just judgement. Anne did not think of questioning that judgement: murder cries out for atonement! She felt that she was guilty before the sea, but she felt no remorse. It was as though she had been brought before a different Judge, almighty and holy as the sea, but not only as just but, like her heart, merciful as well. Hence-forth she could only accept this god become man as her Judge.

But at the judgement seat before which she stood how was Anne to explain this knowledge? How could she dare hope to make the sea, that great, that terrible power, under-stand this? How, when she could not even understand it herself! And what should she offer to her young Duke as atonement for his murder? She did not know. In the pious simplicity of her heart she could neither take responsibility for her action nor explain it—she could only surrender her-self in expiation. In childlike faith she bowed her head.

At that same moment she caught sight of Budoc's dark form rising over the edge of the ship some distance away. Again he appeared to her as a creature of the deep; a messenger of the sea as he had come a short while before.

He climbed on board and came to her. "Come, Anne de Vitré," he said brusquely. "The boat is ready!" His face was sinister and domineering, but his voice sounded quite calm, almost indifferent. Anne felt without fear once more; once more it seemed to her as though Budoc had no power over her. She followed him willingly to the bow of the ship where the boat lay in the water. It was rocking lightly in a sea that seemed suddenly—but gently and joyfully— agitated. Anne felt the breath of a light wind caressing her brow. Dawn was breaking but on the ships all around it was deathly silent. Only from the royal pavilion did there still come the subdued but cheerful murmur of the women's voices.

Budoc bent down silently to help Anne into the boat. She felt his naked arms clasp her knees. He raised her up, high up, as if he were again shouting a jubilant cry of vengeance. It was indeed a cry of vengeance: he was tasting its sweet power to the full. For a few moments Anne hung suspended, motionless, held fast by his arms, over the waves: she had just time to see the much too early rosy glow of sunrise which wreathed the horizon; she could see a sail being hoisted on the distant escort ship which had carried her away from Brittany; it looked like the wing of a swan rising over the waters. Then Budoc let her drop. The waves broke over her with a roar as Anne fell into the sea—down, down into the bottomless depths, where all things can be called by the same name. Then there came the agony of drowning.

In the depths suddenly someone clasped her in his arms

again. She was saved, she was given life—and the roaring lashing waves became quiet as the gentle waves on the strand when they rock a boat. Close to her ears Anne heard a sweet voice, a voice like that of her mother by the cradle of her little brother Alain: it was singing the same song that Anne had sung to the child of the royal murderer. But it sang it to the end.

THE GATE OF HEAVEN

THE GATE OF HEAVEN

THERE was a very curious old document among the archives of my mother's family. No one knew how it had come to be there or what connection it had with the family, for there was no mention in the carefully chronicled history of the family of one of its members having studied astronomy and the natural sciences in Italy in the seventeenth century. And this document originated at that time, and referred to that country and to the study of those subjects. The family called it the "Galilean Document," a highly imaginative designation since there was nothing in it which pointed with any certainty to a connection with Galileo. Only one thing was certain—that the document told of the typical fate of a scientist of those days. The fact that the writer carefully avoided mentioning names, apparently through fear of the Inquisition, which at that time was violently persecuting the followers of the new sciences, was really no justification for the family integrating it into its own history. The fact that my cousin Marianne when travelling in Italy had discovered her own coat of arms among those of former students adorning the halls of the ancient University of Padua, may have provided a possible excuse for this appropriation, but did not throw any light on the mystery of the "Galilean Document." But, like so many similar old writings, it was held in great esteem but hardly ever read.

And so it was that I also got to know its contents for the first time on that memorable night during the Second World War, when my cousin Marianne asked me to fetch the most important documents from the family archives in the old town house where they were in danger of destruction in the bombing, and take them to a safer place. Marianne was spending the war years at my place in the country, but could not very well leave her young children. Her husband, like most of the men of the family, was at the front, and both of us naturally hesitated to entrust the conveyance of these extremely precious documents to strangers. So I decided to go for them myself although well-meaning friends tried to dissuade me because the air-raids on the towns of Germany were becoming more frequent. But it is the way of human nature to imagine horrors of this kind theoretically rather than realistically, and as I, like Marianne, was deeply impressed with the importance of my ancient family and its history, I set off on my mission quite lightheartedly.

The early darkness of autumn had already fallen when I arrived in the town. The railway station seemed strange and a little frightening in its black-out. Of course there were no taxis, so I set off on foot with my small suitcase.

Well, here was my first sight of a blacked-out town. Here amidst the familiar streets with their late-medieval timbered buildings, their baroque mansions and their ancient churches, touched only now and then by the ghostly bluish light of the crawling trams, everything seemed to be masked; everywhere pitch-black windows, and people groping timidly past each other as if they were hurrying, also masked, to some spectral carnival.

And I too was taking part, in my own person, in this spookish carnival. Indeed this general masking was entering into my own inner being, as it were, for I seemed suddenly to lose hold of myself. I felt I had acted quite senselessly in coming to fetch those old documents which a moment before I had regarded as the infinitely precious legacy of centuries; it seemed to me to be not only inevitable but actually reasonable that they should be destroyed, for did not this black-out exemplify and prelude the destruction of my own age and all its traditions? It would not have taken much to make me return to the station without having accomplished my task.

But at this point in my thoughts I found myself already at my destination. I entered the old town house of my relative and was received in a well-lit room by a young man, a distant relative of the family, whom my cousin Marianne had asked to help me sort out and examine the archives. I had already met him on previous visits to the family. He had taken his science degree with distinction and had been working up to the present in the laboratory of an armament works in the town. But now he was being sent to the front;

in fact, he was to set off early in the morning. Therefore we would have to start sorting out the documents straight away. I was more than pleased to fall in with this suggestion and began wondering whether it might not be possible to curtail my stay and actually return to the country late that same night.

When I expressed this hope to the young man, he merely shrugged his shoulders with a dubious air. To tell the truth, I did not take to him. Even his way of speaking—the free and easy jargon of the young generation who have not yet formed their own mode of expression—got on my nerves somewhat. I felt a peculiar and to me hitherto unknown shyness before this self-confident young man. It was as though the natural relation of the different generations towards each other had suddenly been reversed, and I, so much the elder, were in reality the inexperienced person not quite capable of forming a judgement. In a word, I felt in his presence extraordinarily backward and out of date, but at the same time—and this was the peculiar contradiction—a little immature, as though he had experienced things of which I had no inkling. Long forgotten feelings surged back into my mind, the feelings of a young girl who wants to be treated as an adult and feels exasperated when everyone persists in regarding her as if she were still almost a child. For that was just how this young man was treating me; of course quite unconsciously and absolutely as a matter of course. But this was no time to indulge in such feelings, and in any case I was once more fully conscious of the importance of my task, so we set to work.

As the young man had already done some preparatory work, we got on relatively quickly. The vast amount of the documents was the only difficulty. (Good heavens, when a family history covers many centuries, all sorts of things accumulate; and my small suitcase which was all I had brought to carry them, limited what I could take.) So we sorted out only the most important papers, and just as I was locking my suitcase I luckily remembered the "Galilean Document." Marianne, who had a romantic enthusiasm for this document, had specially reminded me to be sure to take it. The young scientist had overlooked it, or rather, he had stowed it away again as being of lesser importance when he saw that it did not concern the family, but now unpacked it again while I informed him briefly of what it was about. On hearing the name Galileo he became keenly alert, looked with interest at the faded pages and said he simply must read them. I reminded him that I wanted to go back by the night train.

"Are you afraid there might be an air-raid?" he asked, without taking his eyes off the manuscript.

"If I were afraid, I certainly wouldn't have come here," I replied frigidly. He laughed, and I felt that he did not believe a word I said. And strangely enough, I did not believe myself either. "My train leaves in half an hour," I added somewhat desperately, "and the manuscript is fairly long."

"Do you know it?" he asked without taking his eyes off the pages. And when I replied that I did not, he said with visible pleasure: "Well, then, it's high time you *did* get to know it." With this he went back to the first page and began to read what I am going to tell you now. For the pages themselves were soon to meet their fate. This is what I heard:

*

I, So-and-So—three crosses followed—the pupil of the esteemed and greatly renowned Master, So-and-So—three more crosses—who have had the honor as well as the grief of knowing the nameless fate of that venerated person in all its details, that is to say, not as the world believes it knows it, but rather, as it really was—I wish to bear testimony to this truth before myself and before coming generations. I wish to bear testimony to it, not only on behalf of the Master but also on behalf of his enemies, or rather, of that enemy who was not his enemy and did not wish to be his enemy, but who became his enemy and had to do so. I refer to that powerful person who brought about the Master's downfall and in doing so himself fell. I shall not anticipate events, however, but shall report everything truthfully in its proper order from the beginning.

I shall begin with that memorable day on which our revered Master set out on his journey to Rome to vindicate himself before the court of the Inquisition. We, his pupils, whom he left behind were still quite confident at that time. Indeed, as is the way of the young, we were presumptuously calm, not only because of our confidence in the superior and inviolable greatness of our Master, but also because of our confidence in that powerful person in Rome whom we were wont to speak of as the patron of our new science. How well I remember the stinging jokes we used to make about the ecclesiastical judges for having dared to summon the Master before their forum. And if we ever worried about our Master, it was because of the hardships of the journey for a man already well on in years, or because of the notorious robbers who infested the highroads of the Papal States and had gotten quite out of hand again since the death of the stern Pope Sixtus. It was only after we had received news of the Master's safe arrival in Rome that I became really troubled about him.

But my anxiety had nothing to do with this news. It had quite a different cause. For that evening Diana, the girl whom I adored and who was privileged to call herself the niece and pupil of our Master, came to visit me for the first time after a long interval, in the top floor room with its open view of the sky which we, the Master's pupils, called "The Gate of Heaven." Here the instruments and lenses with which our Master taught us to search the firmament were kept.

I was so astonished at seeing my adored Diana once again that my hands trembled as I handed her the telescope; and I thought I perceived a slight tremor in her own hands. But I did not dare to ascribe this to my presence for I could never believe that she could ever notice my feelings for her—not to speak of responding to them. Indeed, to my boyish mind she was not just a girl like others, she was almost a goddess. The fact that she was studying something which girls normally did not study made her seem all the more marvellous. My fellow-students jokingly called her Urania, and indeed to me this name seemed the only one worthy of her. For did she not wander beneath the stars like that heavenly muse?

I can still see her intelligent and proud face raised devoutly and solemnly towards the Master, and now and then lighting up as if touched by the radiance of his starry world when, consciously or unconsciously, he gazed into her face as he spoke. But of late, as the journey to Rome drew nearer, she was often pensive and anxious. In the past she used to delight us all by the clever lively questions she would put to the Master (strangely enough she preferred to call him Master rather than Uncle); but now she was absolutely silent during the lectures, and I also noticed that she frequently withdrew to the nearby Convent of the Poor Clares to spend many hours in prayer in their chapel.

On the night of which I speak we were watching for the rise of the planet Jupiter and its four satellites, those famous "Medicean Stars" which, according to the most recent discoveries, rotate around it, and which my German master had sent me to Italy to study. For we Germans too wished to investigate their significance for the position of the earth in the cosmos. Though I had not been long in Italy, I had seen these stars many times, but always indistinctly before, for during the recent period when the Master was still fighting against being summoned to Rome, the sky had been constantly overcast. Only after it had been decided that he must go to Rome had the sky suddenly become so singularly clear that we expected to have the most marvellous view of the planet. And it did indeed rise triumphantly and radiantly, as befitted a kingly constellation, accompanied by its satellites, the "Medicean Stars," which I was now able to observe in perfect clarity for the first time. It seemed to us that the heavens themselves wished to bear testimony for our Master. I had never before felt so convinced of the truth of his findings as on that night. Or was it the proximity of the beloved girl which roused my heart and my mind to this intoxicating enthusiasm?

My beloved too, I felt, was overwhelmed with the same enthusiasm. Though she stood motionless at the telescope, I imagined I could hear her heart beating as wildly as my own. Without looking at her I knew that she was in the same state of tense emotion as I was. At that moment we felt, thought and experienced one and the same thing. True, we had both known for a long while past what these stars signified, but now the knowledge filled our whole being and existence with shattering emotion such as we had never experienced before. It was the moment in which, for the two of us, the old conception of the cosmos finally dissolved, collapsing in a sudden silent fall. Can I say that it collapsed since it had never existed in reality? This earth, this scene of a divine drama of redemption, was not the center of the world. It was an ordinary little planet which humbly circled round the sun with its one moon, just like Jupiter with its "Medicean Stars." An illusion of thousands of years had been blown away like a light curtain caught in a fire, and we fell with open eyes and with everything which we had thought and believed up till then, into the naked infinity of space.

Suddenly Diana uttered a cry. Was it a cry of delight or of horror? This cry defied description. It was simply an attempt to express the inexpressible which we were experiencing. Then she grasped both my hands. It was the first time that we had touched each other.

"So it is true, my friend!" she cried, beside herself. "So it is true! Our Faith no longer has a place in the universe. There are only the eternal laws and we human beings!"

The next moment she lay in my arms, her breast pressed against mine. She had fled to me, and taken refuge in my arms from the terrifying knowledge of the infinity of space. And now it suddenly seemed to me that the infinity of space had changed into the infinity of my adoring love; that its frightening name had been exchanged for a blessed one, and that I had to confess, at once rejoicing and sobbing, my immersion in the beloved.

But Diana quickly straightened up again. She smoothed her tossed hair with both hands and looked at me with an expression in which there was something of the inflexibility of the iron laws of the universe.

"Oh, my friend, my dear friend," she said solemnly. "Now the die is cast: the Master will be condemned. He is lost!"

Saying this she grasped me by the shoulders as if to shake me out of the thrall of my dreams. Her words penetrated slowly into my consciousness, yet they were completely incomprehensible to me. Why? Had we two not recognized just a moment before and with the utmost clarity the truth of the new cosmic picture? How then could the Master be condemned, since this picture represented the truth? I, on the contrary, felt convinced that he could never again be vanquished but rather that his judges were already judged, and I said this to her.

She stroked my hair and forehead tenderly as if I were a child, but her eyes lost nothing of their relentless expression. "It is because it is true that he will be condemned," she said in a low voice. "He will have to be condemned. For have we not seen for ourselves just now that in the immeasurable expanse above us there is no longer a place for the God of our Faith? Or can you imagine that the Son of God came down from heaven just for the creatures on our one little planet? But the Church cannot admit this. She dare not admit it! For it is too terrible!" she added, her voice dropping almost to a whisper. She was trembling with emotion. "We no longer have a God who troubles about us; we have only ourselves now!" And then, almost desperately: "We have only ourselves now, only ourselves! From now onwards man will have to be everything to his fellow-man. But what actually is man, and how will he develop in the ages yet to come?"

And I too was seized with horror. The words of Diana began to terrify me. I came of a deeply devout family and had always been devout myself. (Now that I am no longer a believer I can say this without seeming to praise myself.) And it had never entered my mind that the new conception of the universe which had emerged on my scientific horizon, could interfere with my faith. My German master had always remained a devout Catholic.

"Diana," I cried, "how can you say these . . . these blasphemous things? You're presenting the Church with reasons for condemning our Master, reasons which as you know he himself never admitted she could have. Your Uncle always proved to the Church that one could profess the new science and still be a Christian."

"The Master is deceiving himself," she insisted, "but the Church will not allow herself to be deceived. She will have to condemn the Master. There is no hope for him unless he recants."

This again horrified me. "The Master will never do that," I cried. "Such treachery would cost him his eternal salvation!"

She smiled in a mysterious way. Her eyes, staring and distended with the sheer magnitude of the knowledge, were blue as the distant vault of the night sky. "There is no longer any eternal salvation, my young friend," she whispered, "but neither is there any hell fire. There is only the kind of fire with which they burned Giordano Bruno."

My horror now knew no bounds, for was it not true that women sometimes had second sight? Was it not said that they could tell the future? Oh, God, if I did not love and adore her so unutterably, I would have fled from her now, so greatly did her unbelief terrify me. But of course I could not flee from her. Even the utmost horror could not destroy the charm of her presence; all sensation of horror was immediately submerged in delight, as streams of water disappear in fire.

Meanwhile she was looking at me intently and with a curious air of understanding. "Do you really love me, my young friend," she asked.

As if she did not know the answer! "May I love you, then?" I asked tremulously.

"Yes, you may. I need your love very much. Yes, love me, please love me!" she replied, and sank into my arms once more. Now I no longer felt aware of the horror with which she had just now inspired me, and as I kissed her again and again I spoke no word, and lost, lost utterly all desire to argue with her. We remained clasped in silent embrace for a long time; the narrow garret, "the Gate of Heaven," as we called it, had now really become the gate of Paradise for me.

A few days later the terrible thunderbolt which Diana had foretold fell upon us. I was strolling with the other pupils of the revered Master in the garden of his villa. For we had unanimously decided to wait here for his early return, which we never for a moment doubted. Suddenly we saw a carriage driving in the garden gate. It stopped in front of the villa and two elderly ladies and a young priest got out. While the ladies were asking to see Donna Adriana, the Master's sister, the priest came over to us and asked in a reserved and courteous manner if we were the Master's pupils. Then he informed us briefly and discreetly that his Eminence, naming the Cardinal whom we were wont to refer to as the Master's protector and patron, had instructed him to advise us, in fact to order us, to disperse at once and as unobtrusively as possible; he counselled each of us to return to his own country and his own family. Of course we were shocked at this announcement because it proved definitely that our Master's case was not going well. Actually, he had already been taken to the Palace of the Inquisition. At first we stood thunderstruck, then we began to storm the young priest with questions. But now his face assumed an expression of completely impenetrable reticence, and in brief and stern words he pointed out that he could give us no information concerning the proceedings and decisions of the Holy Office. We knew only too well the truth of that. It was precisely this impenetrable silence regarding current trials which was the most frightening thing about the Inquisition.

While we were standing there dumb with horror, Diana appeared at the door of the villa and beckoned to me. "My friend," she said calmly, "what I said has come to pass. The Master is in the hands of the Inquisition. The Cardinal has advised you and your colleagues to flee. Follow his advice so that you may save the Master's work. I am summoned to Rome. We have to part."

Diana's words made me feel faint with apprehension. The Cardinal had summoned her to Rome. What could that mean? Why had she received different orders from those which we, the Master's pupils, had received? For obviously it was intended to dissociate us from the charge by sending us back to our homes. Was this call to Rome really a summons for Diana? Had she too been accused, and would she, like the Master, have to answer before an ecclesiastical court.

She guessed my thoughts and shook her head. "No, on the contrary," she said, "the instructions given to me are the same as those given to you: I am to go back to my home and family."

"To your home and family?" I repeated, baffled. "But are you not the Master's niece, and is not your home here with him?"

Again she shook her head, and at the same moment put her finger to her lips, for the voices of the strange ladies could be heard in the house. Donna Adriana came and asked Diana to help her to pack her things, because the ladies wanted to set off with her in an hour. She replied that she would be ready immediately, and then, when we were alone once more, she repeated her demand: that I should flee the country and save the Master's work.

"And you?" I asked. "What's to become of you?"

"I will remain near our Master, and if it comes to the worst, I am resolved to share his fate," she said.

"So you too have been denounced to the Inquisition?" I gasped.

"On the contrary," she replied, "the Cardinal is trying to protect me from it, but he can only save you if you obey him. Farewell, my young friend. We must part."

At this I became desperate. "No, I will not leave you," I cried. "Did you not give me permission to love you? Did you not actually invite me to do so? And even if it was

only despair and loneliness which cast you into my arms
. . . what does it matter? I love you! If you want to share
the Master's fate, I want to share yours."

Diana had no time to reply, for just then Donna
Adriana came running back to hurry her up. They went
into the house together, while I set about my own preparations for the journey.

When the two ladies and Diana got into the carriage an
hour later, my servant and I had already mounted our
horses and were standing by ready to follow them. But my
action met with opposition. The two ladies whispered
something to the priest, whereupon he walked up to me
and politely but firmly pointed out that I must obey the
Cardinal's order and return to my own country. In vain I
maintained that the company of myself and my servant
would be a protection for the ladies on their journey. In
order to put an end to the dispute I decided to let the carriage go on alone, but to follow it at a discreet distance.
True, my trick already came to light at the frontier of the
Papal States, where we had to change horses and show our
passes. Now the travelers' indignation at my disobedience
knew no bounds. Of course there were a thousand questions burning on my tongue, but whenever I tried to get
near Diana during the stop at the frontier station, the two
ladies fluttered round her like angry hens around their
chickens, while the young priest punished me by completely
ignoring me. Meanwhile I cherished most wicked desires:
that the carriage might be attacked by bandits while tra-
versing the Papal States, that a wheel might break, that we

might meet the wild bulls of the Campagna. I shouldn't have minded what it was if only it gave me an opportunity of protecting Diana. Yes, my youthful mind revelled in such possibilities.

And actually, we were only a few miles inside the frontier of the Papal States when I became aware that the noise of the carriage, which had disappeared round a wooded corner, was no longer audible. Instead, I heard a wild uproar and terrified cries for help. My servant and I spurred on our horses, and as we galloped around the edge of the wood we saw some bandits pulling the baggage off the coach from which they had made the travelers dismount. We fired our pistols and the ruffians disappeared into the thicket as if the ground had swallowed them. While my servant was helping the coachman to load up the luggage again, I at last succeeded in speaking to Diana alone for a moment.

"I knew you would follow me," she said, "and I've been very troubled about you. But this attack has been an unexpected bit of good luck. After this incident the Cardinal will receive you with open arms and try to protect you, because he loves me very much. Tell him everything you told me up in the Gate of Heaven. Convince him that one can profess the new knowledge of the universe and still be true to the Church. You cannot serve the Master better than by doing so, and in any event you will save yourself by this. And you must not grieve if we have to be parted in Rome at first. It is not important that you speak to me, but it *is* important that you speak to the Cardinal."

During the remainder of the journey the two ladies and the young priest showed themselves completely altered in their attitude towards me. The former thanked God without ceasing for having sent me to their aid at the right moment, while the young priest offered not only to procure suitable lodgings for me in Rome, but also to introduce me to his superior the Cardinal, who he knew would be deeply grateful to me for the protection I had given to Donna Diana. Thus it was that we arrived in Rome on the best of terms with each other.

First there were a few days of waiting, and I spent them exploring the Eternal City. Just then all Rome was seething with excitement over the fabulously magnificent state entry of the new Polish ambassador to the Holy See. Everyone was talking about his Arab horses with their golden shoes, and the silver armour and richly embroidered purple saddle-cloths of his horsemen. I was more than surprised to note that the people of this holy city were so eager for spectacles and so blatantly worldly. I learned moreover from the ambassador of my own king, to whom I introduced myself at once, that the Cardinals vied with each other in staging magnificent plays and operas—in short, that this city of Rome, which I had pictured as enveloped in the sombre radiance of religious zeal, wallowed in all the beauties and frivolities of the world. Luxurious palaces were being built everywhere, and the ruins of the palaces and baths of the Early Romans were being plundered to help build them. The common people stood about and stared, and seemed to find pleasure in all these doings. I also saw enchanting fountains decorated with stone statues of creatures from pagan times, whose shell-shaped horns dipped into the bubbling water, while real little boys shouted with glee as they rode on the backs of marble dolphins. I was also thrilled by the sight of the proud cavalcades of Papal nobles, specially the favorites of the reigning Pope, who I was told were the most powerful men in Rome next to the Pope himself. Coming from Germany, a poor country torn by decades of religious wars, this display of wealth and magnificence was at first painful and surprising, the more so since I noticed that nobody here was interested in the bitter sufferings of my country. Even the young priest with whom I had traveled and who meanwhile had revealed himself as the private chaplain of the Cardinal, with whom he was arranging an audience for me, listened with visible inattention when I told him of the great German war. However, the prevalent cheerful worldliness restored me to a certain calm and confidence, especially when I thought of my Master's trial. For I deemed it impossible that Rome, so absorbed in splendors and festivities, could really take the Inquisition as seriously as I had been informed it was being taken.

Meanwhile the young priest had kept his word and in a few days I received the promised summons to an audience with His Eminence. I had expected to find cheerful crowds of singers and actors in his palace, but it was not like that. The apartments through which I was conducted were austere and lonely—they breathed that atmosphere of sad renunciation which I remembered in my own country in the homes of bishops and church dignitaries which my father frequented and where I often accompanied him. Finally I was conducted to a room which was full of the most varied assortment of instruments all quite familiar to me. There was a globe on the table, and maps of the firmament showing the constellations were spread about beside it. There was no doubt but that the inmate of this room was intimately acquainted with my own science.

The Cardinal entered the room. As I had expected, he was a fine and distinguished looking gentleman, with a resolute and reticent facial expression. His beard, cut to a point in the fashion of the time, lent him a certain air of a man of the world and reminded me of paintings and sketches of our generals in the time of the great German wars. But that was not what surprised me most in his appearance. Some resemblance in the eyes and forehead so staggered me that I was hardly able to keep from staring at him. I could not have been more bewildered if I had been suddenly confronted with Diana herself.

The Cardinal stretched out his hand that I might kiss his ring, then began speaking to me in the friendly and debonair tone of a man of the world. By right he should be very angry with me, he said, because I had thrown his well-meant advice to the winds and come to Rome instead of returning to my own country. But the gratitude which he owed me for protecting his niece made good everything else, and he was eager to express this gratitude—Providence sometimes made use even of an act of disobedience to serve its good purpose, and he did not wish to be less magnanimous than Providence. When the Cardinal mentioned his niece a very tender and gentle expression lit up his face; although very little in accord with the air of detachment proper to a priest, it made him all the more attractive as a man. The cause for anxiety which had made him decide that I should leave the country had not been removed, he continued, and now that I was in Rome there was no other way for me to avoid certain difficulties which threatened me as a prominent pupil of my Master, than to avail myself of the protection which his own home afforded. He hoped I would not mind pretending to be his secretary for a time. For I must surely have noticed, from the equipment in his room, that his niece's love of astronomy was a family trait. As he spoke these last words a very human and tender expression crossed the churchman's face once more. He himself would find great pleasure in my company, he concluded, for he had learned that I had also been the pupil of a very famous German master about whom he would like to know more.

These last remarks made me listen attentively, for did they not betray that the Cardinal's own opinions were close to those of the Master? He appeared to read my thoughts, for he suddenly said: "Yes, those are great hypotheses, my young friend, very daring hypotheses." It seemed to me that by these last words he meant to show me how I myself should word such findings. But immediately afterwards he involved me in such a lively discussion of these same hypotheses that I felt he himself must be just as convinced as I of the correctness of my teacher's views.

And so I was accepted into the Cardinal's household, and just as I had worked hitherto with my Master's instruments, now I worked with the Cardinal's; I had full authority to use them and, more important still, to write down the results of my observations and give them to the Cardinal as opportunity occurred. I soon noticed that I could speak very candidly about my Master's scientific knowledge; the Cardinal actually demanded this frankness and listened to me without contradiction. In fact, he sometimes added a jocularly assenting comment to my statements. Once he commented that it might be very salutary to human pride to consider that the earth was not in the center of the universe but just a very small insignificant planet. And though he introduced the words "great hypotheses" from time to time into our discussions as though they were meant as a kind of warning, he never set himself against my range of ideas. But as soon as I tried to change the subject from my Master's scientific knowledge to his trial, he broke off the conversation, and though, as a gentleman and an aristrocrat, he would never hurt my feelings by ordering me to be silent, he made me feel clearly that there was a limit here which I dare not overstep.

During this time I neither saw nor heard anything of Diana, and the Cardinal's chaplain discreetly but firmly opposed my wish to pay my respects to her and to her two traveling companions, pointing out that I was not permitted to move one step from the Cardinal's palace. It gradually dawned on me that I was more or less a prisoner, that I was probably under the surveillance of the Inquisition, and that Diana too, as a pupil of the Master, was very probably also a kind of prisoner, but that thanks to the magnanimity of the Cardinal we were being detained under a sort of chivalrous house arrest. For although I was forbidden to go out, within the precincts of the palace I enjoyed complete freedom, and could show myself and move about without the least constraint. Every morning I attended the early Mass which the Cardinal celebrated in his private chapel in the presence of numerous aristocrats from the neighboring palaces. I was frequently invited to dine with him, and on these occasions the conversation of one or other of the guests promptly turned to my science, and I soon noticed to my great astonishment that my Master had many wellwishers among the higher clergy of Rome. Indeed, I could hardly believe that an Inquisition existed in the midst of this enlightened and noble Roman society, and even when I remembered the fate of Giordano Bruno, which Diana had recalled and lamented that eventful evening in the Gate of Heaven, it all seemed to me like a fantastic tale. To be sure, the company around His Eminence's table did not remain silent concerning the Church's objections to the discoveries of the new science, but I welcomed these objections for the opportunity which they gave me of zealously asserting that one truth could not possibly disprove another. In fact, I allowed myself to be so carried away as to express the passionate conviction that the newly discovered astronomical picture would reveal the Creator to mankind in even greater glory. They listened to me in silence but not, I imagined, without good-will. In my youthful inexperience I did not guess that this conversation at the dinner-table was a kind of cross-examination, and I surrendered myself freely to the joyful consciousness that I was hastening to the aid of my esteemed Master and at the same time earning Diana's praise. Indeed, this thought lent a secret enchantment to all these conversations and afforded my youthful heart a mystical fulfillment of its innocent love which compensated me again and again for the physical separation from my beloved. The Cardinal too was included in this secret and enchanting region of my thoughts, for I knew now that Diana was the child of his sister, the one woman whom he had loved and honored supremely and whom he now continued to love in her daughter. He had no desire to lavish his affection on favorites as the other Cardinals did, and his tender father's love for this niece had nothing ostentatious or worldly about it; it had never seduced him into ambitious plans of marriage for her. He had given way, with understanding and unselfishness, to her "love of the stars," as he called it, and had entrusted her to the Master though under the protective pretence that she was related to the latter.

But to return to the dinner-table conversation of my fellow-guests. One day, when I was dining with the Cardinal once more, I observed among the guests, all high church dignitaries, a shabbily attired and extremely ascetic-looking priest. I took him for one of those poor priests without a living of whom Rome was full, and thought the Cardinal had probably invited him out of pity. He ate his meal in silence and did not contribute one word to the conversation, which this time too had turned on the usual subject. But it did strike me that the mood was somehow different today—there was a certain hint of uneasiness, and I did not know the reason for it.

"Well," one of the prelates said to me, "I agree with you that belief in the Creator can only gain in majesty and glory through the new astronomical discoveries. But what then about the Redemption? Is it conceivable that God sent His only-begotten Son down to this miserable little planet, as your Master teaches that the earth is?"

"In the Redemption God reveals Himself to man; the belief in the Redemption can never be shaken by the heavenly bodies; it can only be shaken by man's failure."

At these words the silent ascetic looked up. "You're right, young man," he said. "But man is weak, he should not be so presumptuous as to question God about mysteries which in His wisdom He keeps hidden from us." He said this in a low, indeed an almost feeble voice, yet all the others instantly ceased speaking. It was almost as though they were holding their breath.

"We do not question God," I replied, "we question nature."

"Nature is a pagan," replied the ascetic. "The great master Aristotle knew how to cope with her. We have reason to be grateful to him, for where would we end up if everyone started investigating on his own? A hundred years ago someone started interpreting the Bible on his own, and this has resulted in the schism within the Church. I fear that a breach between the world of God and the world of man may result from the present developments.

Are you never afraid, young man, that you scientists may be deceiving yourselves?"

"Our apparatus and instruments are impartial," I replied, "they do not deceive us; they have neither fear nor ambition; they tell the truth."

"But your replies contradict Holy Scripture," said the ascetic. "For instance, it is stated in the Bible: 'The sun stood still in the midst of heaven'—not—'The earth stood still.' "

"I do not understand what that means," I replied candidly. "The Bible is not a text-book of natural science. I know that God is and always will be the Lord of creation, no matter how much I know or don't know about creation."

"Well said!" cried the Cardinal. "To young people like this one the new conception of the universe will not be dangerous." With these words he turned to the ascetic.

"And even if it should prove dangerous to youth in the beginning," I cried passionately, "must one not nevertheless respect truth?"

Now the Cardinal retreated. "Yes, that's the great question," he said, hesitantly, "only it can be put in another way: Can something be the truth when it contradicts the Faith."

I was about to reply: "Can something be opposed to the Faith when it is the truth?" But now the ascetic joined in again: "The Holy Church decides what is the truth," he said looking at me sharply. At this I remained silent, and the whole company fell into an awed silence too.

That same evening the Cardinal's young chaplain came to me. "Do you know that you were before the Inquisition, so to speak, today?" he asked. "The silent guest was none other than the Censor of the Holy Office."

"Have I prejudiced the Master's cause?" I asked, in alarm.

He put his finger to his lips, but it struck me that he looked quite confident.

Just then there seemed some little hope that I might see Diana again, for one morning I caught sight of her two traveling companions at the Cardinal's early Mass. I went up to them after Mass and their greeting proved at once that they were still very kindly disposed towards me. They whispered to me with such animation that their black mantillas fluttered, that Diana was well but was living with them in complete retirement which could only be relaxed if or when a certain plan of the Cardinal's had matured sufficiently to be divulged. Then they introduced me to a young French marquis, saying he was a relative of theirs, and told him how I had protected them on their journey, whereupon the young Frenchman shook hands with me, though somewhat condescendingly.

Although the hints thrown out by the ladies were so vague, they aroused my hopeful expectations. But the riddle was soon to be solved.

A few days later, when I was summoned to dinner by

the Cardinal once more, I found the latter on the balcony focusing the telescope for the Marquis. As I entered the room he came over to me and said: "Today we are celebrating my niece's engagement by a little banquet from which you, dear friend, could not possibly be absent. For do we not owe it to you that we can celebrate it at all?" With these words, which obviously referred to my rôle of protector, he turned towards the Marquis, who shook hands with me again in his rather condescending manner.

Now, God knows I had never imagined that I had any claim on my beloved, not to speak of any hope that I would one day take her home as my bride. I simply could not picture my queen of the stars, my Urania, as I used to call her in my boyish enthusiasm, as a married woman at all. Hence His Eminence's news struck me like a thunderbolt—in vain I struggled to utter the words which were obviously expected of me. At this moment, however, the door opened and Diana came in, accompanied by the two companions of her journey. Like them she wore the beautiful court dress which Roman etiquette prescribed for ladies—the black lace mantilla beneath which her face looked small, pale and passionately excited.

The Cardinal went up to her, took her by the hand, and with a fatherly air led her up to the Marquis.

"Here, my dear niece," he said, "is the husband whom I have chosen for you. May your future marriage be blessed."

But now something quite unexpected and unheard of happened, Diana, who had turned very pale at the Cardinal's words, withdrew her hand from his. "Your Eminence," she said with a gesture expressing pride, dignity and that iron determination which I had known in her since our time together up in the Gate of Heaven, "I am unable to consent to your choice, for I have already chosen my fate: There is only one man in the whole world whom I would follow to the ends of the earth, even if that means to imprisonment and death."

I do not know if she really spoke these last words, or if they passed into my spirit from the depths of hers. I only know that I felt the scales fall from my eyes. She loved the Master, the prisoner, the man who was probably in danger of death! And now I realized that I had always known that she loved him and him alone, and that this accounted for the indescribable fascination of her whole being, which my love had apprehended as the perfume of one and the same flower blooming in the depths of the hearts of both of us.

We all stood as if paralyzed by Diana's refusal. Then, with the debonair self-command of a man of the world the Cardinal turned to the young Frenchman. "I fear we have frightened my niece, Monsieur le Marquis," he said. "We have sprung it on her too abruptly. Will you please excuse a churchman, who is ill equipped to act the part of father to a young girl."

"On the other hand, I ask you to excuse me, Your Eminence," replied the Marquis. "I am not accustomed to playing the rôle of the rejected person." Saying this, he bowed with icy formality, and left the room. The Cardinal signed to Diana's startled chaperons, who thereupon followed the Marquis out, apparently to appease him. I expected the Cardinal to dismiss me too, but he had obviously forgotten all about me.

"My child," he said, turning to Diana, "do you realize that you are not at all safe in Rome? The Marquis wished to give you the protection of his name and his country. You have just now thwarted a plan which I had set my heart upon, for the sake of your safety and your future. It will not be easy to take it up again."

"Do not take it up again, Your Eminence," she cried passionately. "I beseech you not to—it would be useless. You have no control over my future."

He looked at her with growing surprise. "Do you deny my right to look after you, Diana?" he asked gravely. "Up till now the daughters of Christian Rome have not desired to choose their husbands for themselves. What has brought you to this mood of insubordination?"

She did not answer, but her silence emitted a highly alarming challenge. The Cardinal did not take his eyes off her. Suddenly his expression became uncannily alert: he had grasped that Diana was no longer a daughter of Christian Rome.

"Have you also seen the 'Medicean Stars,' Diana?" he asked her suddenly. Then, without waiting for her reply, he turned towards the telescope which he had adjusted for the Marquis a little time before, and signed to her to come out on the balcony. Suddenly she began to tremble. At the same time her face took on that inexorable expression which it had worn that time up in the Gate of Heaven. A nameless fear came over me. I felt that we were on the edge of an abyss—that Diana was capable of divulging her apostasy to the Cardinal. Had she gone mad? Anyone else in my place would have thought that she had. I knew better. Her whole aim was to destroy every possibility of contracting this hated marriage; she would prefer to fall a victim to the Inquisition. But was she not aware that in doing so she would be condemning the beloved Master too? On the other hand, she had never counted on his being saved. This loss of faith on her part was something much more terrible than I had suspected up till now; it was sheer despair. For to abandon faith in God—at this moment I realized it for the first time—meant forsaking the very fundament of life; it meant forsaking life itself.

Meanwhile she had gone up to the telescope which the Cardinal had adjusted for her. Now she looked through it. As she did so she trembled more and more; it was as though a silent storm were blowing from universal space down upon a young tree, which had already been uprooted. She surrendered herself to it without resistance. Slowly, almost solemnly, she covered her face with her hands. The gesture expressed an admission. The Cardinal understood it.

"Why do those stars frighten you, my child?" he asked gently. "Are you horrified by the cold infinity of the universe? Can you no longer recognize God the Father in it, just as you no longer recognize me?"

The abyss had been reached. The next moment it would swallow up every bit of confidence in the Master's cause which I had built up within myself while in this house.

Then the Cardinal said: "Perhaps you think, Diana, that yonder infinity could wreck your faith? Is it a universe without God which you imagine you see, and which you acknowledge? In that case the work of your Master, and indeed even he himself, would be inimical to the Church, and would therefore have to be judged and condemned by us."

It was the first time that the Cardinal had mentioned the Master's trial in my presence. "Answer me, my child," he ordered. His voice did not sound severe, but it could not be ignored. Suddenly I remembered having heard that at trials of the Inquisition the Cardinal had strictly forbidden the application of torture because he was able to extract all necessary admissions solely by the influence of his personality and his commanding will.

But the application of these powers was not necessary here. Diana had no intention of evading a confession. She stood erect and proud as though she had become a new, a free person.

"And if that were so, Your Eminence, if the Master were really declared to be an enemy of the Church," she asked passionately, "should not the Church draw him, her enemy, to her heart? Should she not love him? Would not this be the only true defeat of defection which would remain open to her, and at the same time the only ratification by Him whose vicegerent on earth she believes herself to be."

"The Church loves, my child, even when she judges, but it is not for you to judge the Church," he replied.

As he said this a diabolical expression crossed her face.

It happened quickly as lightning, yet nevertheless it seemed to span space. Her pain over her lost faith took refuge in hatred of that faith. "Then it was love which made you burn Giordano Bruno?" she cried. "Oh, in that case I'm glad to be free of you and your Church! The day will certainly come when the same things which you are doing now will be done to you. This same science which you are seeking to destroy, will destroy you."

The Cardinal turned deathly pale at her words. "You are right, my child," he said. "You are perfectly right. If faith in God is extinguished, the world will lose all fear." He hesitated for a moment. I felt he was about to come to a decision and that its nature was inevitable in view of what had been said.

"Your Eminence," I besought him raising my hands in pleading, "spare your niece, forgive her, if she is not yet able to cope with the new conception of the universe, but ..." I was going to say: "She will be in time," only he did not allow me to finish speaking but motioned to me imperiously to be silent. Now he was no longer the kindly confidant of my youthful enthusiasm, nor the sympathizer with my scientific knowledge and the fond guardian of Diana. He was now only the prince of the Church.

"You too are right, my friend," he said calmly, "my niece is not able to understand the new conception of the universe. She never will be, for man as such is unable to comprehend it. Kindly accompany Donna Diana to her litter. The ladies will be waiting for her."

I noticed that he neither held out his hand for her to

kiss his ring, nor gave her his blessing. She made no effort to soften him. Perhaps she had not even noticed the lack of these favors. She was intensely agitated and almost fainting with exhaustion, and willingly allowed me to lead her away.

When we came out of the palace there was no sign of the litter. I asked the porter, and he told me that the ladies had already been taken home in it but had promised to send it back at once. Diana had walked farther into the courtyard which, like all Roman courtyards, was filled with the sharp aroma of the thick laurel bushes. I followed her, full of apprehension: she would surely wake up at any moment to a realization of her terrible position. But my apprehension was unfounded. When she turned her face towards me in the dazzling moonlight I noticed that it bore an expression of joyful intoxication.

"I'm free, I'm free!" she whispered breathlessly. "I have shattered that terrible project for my marriage! The Cardinal can hardly present a heretic to the Marquis for a wife. This was what I wanted, just what I wanted! Do rejoice with me young friend, do be happy with me!"

"I cannot be happy," I replied. "Oh, Diana, how can you risk your life like that? I would die of fear on your account did I not know that the Cardinal loves you so dearly."

She did not take any notice of this last remark, but only looked at me once with her rapturous expression. "Surely you don't think that I would wish to live in safety if the Master perishes?" she asked.

I replied that I still hoped he would be safe, and that I based my hope on the discussions I had had with the Cardinal himself regarding the new scientific knowledge, and the fact that it could not conflict with our Faith.

She tenderly stroked my forehead and hair just as she had done up in the Gate of Heaven. "So you're still the same, my guileless young friend! But remain like that. Try to save yourself by remaining with the Cardinal, because one of us must survive to continue the Master's work. I've told you that already. This work must never be lost. It is your task to carry it into the future. Promise me that you will do so!"

"I promise everything that you wish, beloved," I stammered, "but. . . ."

"Why do you call me 'beloved'?" she interrupted. "You know, do you not, that I belong to another?"

"I have always known that you do not belong to me," I replied, "but that does not prevent me from loving you. Do you not understand that it makes one happy to spend oneself in love, even though it be in vain?"

"Oh, yes," she said softly. "Yes, I do understand. The Master does not love me either. He loves only his stars. And it's right that way, for him as well as for me. But for you, my young friend, it must be different." Again she stroked my hair tenderly.

"No," I replied passionately, "it's right this way for me

too; I love my secret happiness, which is like yours. We two can never be disappointed in our love."

Now she looked at me with her great eyes and there was love in them. "How good it is to hear you say that," she whispered, "and how sadly I have undervalued you! Forgive me for not having known you better. Now we are brother and sister by our love. Yes, indeed, we are closely related by the mutual fullness of our heart's love in the midst of all those other people who will never understand us. Oh, how crude and selfish the love of most people is! But you are my brother."

She put her arms around me just as she had done up in the Gate of Heaven, and I put my arms around her. And now I felt convinced that our united love would bring us not only a brotherly and sisterly happiness, but also a deep sense of security in the midst of whatever fate should hold for us.

We were only startled from this intimate parley by the sound of approaching footsteps. A servant informed us that the litter was ready, but when we went over to it we noticed at once that it was not the one we were waiting for.

"His Eminence has sent his own," the servant told us as he opened the door adroitly for Diana to enter. And here again this little door seemed to open up a whole fresh page of destiny. I felt an intense desire to accompany my beloved, but I was forbidden to leave the palace, and today particularly it would not do to anger the Cardinal any more.

But the open door of the litter seemed to frighten Diana

too. "Oh, my God," she said, "it's as narrow and stuffy in there as in a prison! It's almost like a coffin!" She visibly shrank from getting in.

"Would you not prefer to wait for the ladies' litter to come back?" I asked. But now she was smiling again, and looking at me once more with that rapturous expression she said quickly: "No, no, this or any other litter will take me to the same end! Farewell, my young friend, and remember your task." Then she nimbly stepped into the litter, the servant shut the door and pulled forward the bearing shaft, and before Diana had time to draw back the window curtain to wave good-bye to me, the bearers set off at a run. I was overcome with longing for another glimpse of the beloved girl, and at the same time a dreadful fear overwhelmed me. "Stop! Stop!" I cried running after the bearers, but they did not hear me. They had already reached the gateway of the courtyard, and the next moment had disappeared from sight.

When I returned to the palace there was an oppressive silence and air of abandonment in the passages and on the stairways; all the residents seemed to have retired. There was nothing left for me but to do the same. First, however, I had to carry out my nightly task of locking the observatory to safeguard the instruments kept there. I entered the room through an adjacent chamber, the heavy carpeting of which muffled my footsteps. The candles had been extinguished in both rooms and it was dark inside save for the bluish Roman moon which was shining in through the windows, lighting up the outlines of the big heavy pieces of furniture which stood out in the darkness like mountain ridges. The whole room looked peculiarly unfamiliar and spectral. I went in quickly and was going towards the balcony to carry in the telescope, but when I got to the middle of the room I noticed that the Cardinal was there. He was sitting with bowed head, his hands before his face; his whole form, wrapped in its crimson robe, looked in the darkness as if he had thrown a cloak of mourning about him. The moonlight touched only his beautiful strong hands, so often raised in benediction. It was as though they too, like everything else in the room, were hovering over a spectral abyss.

I stood still, greatly startled, and was about to withdraw hurriedly, but I had already been seen. The crouching figure let his hands drop from his face, which now suddenly, like his hands, gave an impression of utter helplessness. His whole appearance was that of one who, after the utmost exertions, allows weakness to overcome him—and in such a state a man should not be seen by another, unless he does not mind being the object of unutterable pity.

"Pardon me, Your Eminence, I didn't mean to take you by surprise," I stammered. Involuntarily I knelt down, it was an assurance of my respect which I felt I should offer to this afflicted man, more particularly now, in the hour of his weakness. Minutes passed. I did not dare to move. The room lost its daytime aspect more and more. The Cardinal remained in his despondent posture.

At last he made a movement. "You did not take me by surprise," he said in a weary tone. "I was waiting for you —I felt the need to speak with a human being. Stand up and tell me truly what you think of it all."

Even in this moment of greatest weakness his order seemed to have a compelling force. Nevertheless, I was only able to partially comply with it. "I beg Your Eminence to allow me to remain kneeling," I said. "It is the most suitable posture, because I am hoping for your mercy."

"And what do you mean by that, my friend?" he asked.

"Oh, Your Eminence," I cried. "You know it as well as I do. Your heart demands of you at this moment just what mine does."

"My heart," he replied, "has only to be silent in this case, and I may say, to suffer. You are a believer, a faithful son of the Church, and you must know that."

Yes, I did indeed know it, but had he not said: "I was waiting for you, I felt the need to speak with a human being?" By God, he would find one. For now I decided to dare all. "Your Eminence, I love your niece," I said. "I adore her. She is the most precious being I know on earth."

Now for the first time he straightened up, and the moonlight lit his face more brightly. "Then I have to save you too, my poor young friend," he said. "I understand your pain, and I am not ashamed to admit that I share it. But there is something greater than the pain of love—there is the sacrifice of the one most dear to us." At these words his voice became infinitely tender, and yet I felt as though we were advancing as we spoke into a region as cold as cosmic space.

"No, Your Eminence," I cried, "there is nothing greater than love! If your niece denied her faith she did so in order to share the Master's fate. Acquit him and she will find her way back to the Faith, for the Master himself, Your Eminence, has never lost the Faith. Believe my declaration, I beg of you. Do please believe me."

He did not contradict me. "Why should I not believe you?" he said calmly. "You are thoroughly worthy of confidence. I do not hesitate to say that you are a valuable find for us priests. Your friendship has proved a great happiness to me, but it would be a grave error to imagine one could judge mankind in general by you. It is true that neither the new cosmic picture nor the new investigation of natural phenomena can be injurious to the true believer. But who are the true believers?"

"You are one, Your Eminence," I replied fearlessly.

At this he made a gesture which was almost like a stern repudiation, and said: "I have been given the task of protecting the faithful. I have taken on the duty of suppressing everything which could harm them."

"Can one protect the Faith by suppressing what endangers it?" I retorted.

"You think I am a man of little faith," he replied calmly. "You think that because I cannot be confident that the Christian world will be able to stand up to the new cosmic picture and the new science."

I did not venture an answer, but silence can be an answer too. The Cardinal understood this at once. "It's true," he said, "I *am* weak in faith. In your sense we priests have always been weak in faith, for we have always persecuted and exterminated heretics. We have done this although our Lord and Master has told us to let the cockle and the wheat grow together until the time of harvest. We have never followed that instruction. We could not follow it, else the cockle would have choked the wheat long ago. We shall not be able to follow it even now."

At his last words I had fallen on my knees once more. Again he made a gesture of stern reprimand. "Do stand up," he said impatiently. "Your Master has no need of your intercession. I have acquitted him long ago in my heart. But there are people who, though themselves inviolable, are dangerous vessels of corruption for others. You may be sure that other stars will follow these 'Medicean Stars.' Terrible stars will arise in the firmament of mankind. . . ."

At these words his eyes opened wide and looked almost white in the moonlight as though a spectral light were illuminating them. I had the impression that he was seeing a vision. After a little time he continued in a gentle but resolute voice: "I have now seen the human being of the future. Just as that unhappy girl has brought about her own destruction, the human race will one day bring about the destruction of the world. For knowledge will always be paid for by death. It was so in Eden with the first man and woman, and it will always be so."

"And nevertheless, dear Eminence," I said, "you yourself are a man of the future, for you too have accepted the new view of the universe."

He did not disavow this. It was one of those moments when a man stands fully revealed to his fellow man. Every barrier of age and station which divided us had fallen.

"To be sure," he said, "I have accepted the new view of the universe, but do you think, perchance, that it is in no way dangerous for me to have done so? After all, what do you layfolk know of us clergy? What is your private mental picture of us? Have you any conception of the abyssmal temptation to which the bearers of the powers of the priesthood are a prey? Have you even the barest inkling of the inward struggles with which we have to contend in complete and deadly loneliness, without any claim on the authoritative assurances and solaces which you are wont to receive from us? It certainly did not require the new science to teach us this. I assure you it is not only the victims of the Inquisition who are martyrs, but also we, who condemn them. For it is difficult to prepare a place for the Eternal on earth; to make the supernatural and the invisible a certainty. Revelation lies far more than a thousand years behind us, and what do the few miracles and spiritual favors which have been granted us in the internal signify? Who can assure us that even these did not rest on pious illusions? Or are we in ourselves, perchance—I mean the persons composing the visible Church—an incontrovertible testimony? Do you know the history of the Church? Do you know the causes of the Reformation? What are your thoughts when you contemplate the ostentation and splendour of the Rome of today? Does it really give you the impression that the Kingdom of Christ exists here? Are we not entangled in all the affairs of this world? Is there any political intrigue in which we have not a hand, are not perhaps obliged to have a hand? To be sure, there are holy monasteries in which poverty and renunciation are zealously practiced; I mention but one, the Oratory of Divine Love.* In the midst of the world there are hidden souls of the purest piety, but are not all these like shipwrecked people clinging to a solitary plank in the raging sea of this world? Are they not like Peter, who tried to walk on the waves, and sank?"

While he was saying all these things in a low monotonous voice I had the feeling that with each word he was separating himself farther from me; that he too was walking on abyssmal waves, his form and his spirit colored to the point of unrecognizability by the ghostly light of the moon, and that I was following him over the abysses of the night. And yet, was not it too—the night and its strange light—real as real could be?

At last the Cardinal fell silent; he had reached, as it were, the darkest peak of night and now remained standing on its pinnacle.

"But Peter didn't sink when he walked on the waves," I said. "He grasped the hand of Christ."

He looked at me almost angrily, then said, again in his low monotonous voice: "And how do you think that we

---

*The Oratory of St. Philip Neri, founded in Rome in 1548.

should grasp Christ's hand? Where is that hand at this moment of ours?" His eyes remained fixed upon me; again I recalled his prohibition of torture: I perceived his inner power of extracting admissions. At the same time I felt certainties which had been buried in my subconscious up till then, suddenly opening up within me under the influence of his eyes.

"Do you not think it is possible, Your Eminence," I said, "that one should simply leave the safety of the Faith in the hands of God, even if the dangers of the world threaten to engulf it?"

"And how do you envisage this leaving of the Faith in the hands of God—I mean in the case in question?"

"If you stay the arm of the Inquisition and save the Master, and if you pardon your niece, that will be a complete victory for the Faith, and at the same time a triumph for the new truth, which you yourself accept."

There was a long and pregnant silence. His face, which a few moments before had been unrecognizable because of the anguish of the night, became slowly more distinct now. The look of suffering seemed to have completely disappeared. Bleak, unfamiliar and infinitely lonely, it almost resembled the moon landscaped beyond in the heavens, and I felt I should never be able to reach him again.

"Your Eminence," I implored, "will you deign to answer me just one single question? Can you imagine, can you bear to think that the Faith will be saved by a manifest untruth?"

Another long silence followed. Would I not receive an

answer? Involuntarily I closed my eyes at the thought of this possibility. When I opened them again the Cardinal had left the room.

During the next two days I hoped in vain that the unfinished conversation would be resumed. To tell the truth, in my heart I knew very well that this would not happen, but I was too young to be resigned to a lost hope. Besides, my high opinion of the Cardinal revolted against the thought that he could really make a decision contrary to his better judgement. Meanwhile I did not see him again in the observatory, and he did not invite me to dine with him. To my enquiry as to whether I might pay my respects to him, his personal servant replied that His Eminence was attending important court sessions. Neither was the chaplain to be seen; he was probably in attendance on the Cardinal. The palace was strangely deserted those days. And in that desertion I became obsessed with the fear that a decision was pending in the Master's trial by the Inquisition.

At last, on the third day, I met the chaplain on the stairs. He tried to pass me quickly, but I grabbed him by his cassock. He looked at me sadly and evasively. "For God's sake tell me how things are going with the Master?" I gasped.

"You know I must not speak about it," he replied gravely.

"Does that mean that there is no hope for him?" I cried beside myself. My anxiety touched his heart, for in all truth he too was suffering.

"Unless he recants," he replied sadly.

"Never! Never! That would be betrayal! That would be a barefaced lie!" I cried.

He gave me a strange look. "Ah, what does a lie mean here and in these times?" he said in a low voice. Then, hurriedly freeing himself from my grasp, he said: "Well, let us pray for your Master, let us pray for him." And he was gone.

Once more I was alone in the oppressively silent palace. Everything now seemed changed to my eyes. The observatory was deserted, robbed of its meaning. Even the architecture of the house spoke a different language from before. It struck me as ostentatious and facade-like, just as though the gestures of these garish pillars and flights of steps were concealing a secret but deep uncertainty which was unable to face the sober reality. "What does a lie mean here and in these times?" the young priest had said. Did he believe in condemning truth? Did he believe in the Master's recantation? I could not bear it any longer, I had to know what was happening.

During the night, being unable to sleep, I planned a desperate action. I had ascertained that the Cardinal and his chaplain went out very early each morning. So I waited until the carriage drove off, then stole into the chaplain's room, took a cassock from a cupboard, and put it on. In this disguise I succeeded in slipping out of the palace unnoticed, for the servants, who were taking things easy in their master's absence, were not as watchful as usual. I remembered where the Palace of the Inquisition was from my first day's wandering alone about Rome, and I reached it without difficulty. A few high prelates had just arrived at the gateway; their elegant litters and carriages were crowded around the entrance. I mingled with their attendants and pushed my way along with the throng through a long gloomy passage. A very young and wildly excited Dominican friar came rushing along towards us. He gave a searching look over my companions, then to my horror fixed his eyes on me.

"You belong to Archbishop . . . .'s suite," he said, mentioning a name completely unknown to me. Please follow me into the box on the left." Without waiting for my answer he hurried on, again at a run, down the gloomy corridor. On reaching the end he opened a door and invited me to enter.

"You know what you're to do," he said. I had no idea what he meant, but he had already shut the door behind him.

I found myself in a small, narrow chamber, with a little glass window. I went up to the window, pushed back the glass and looked into a big hall, in which an ecclesiastical court was just assembling for a solemn session. I saw a long table covered in black with a crucifix on it. A candle was burning at each side of the crucifix. But these candles only seemed to accentuate the gloom of the hall rather than illuminate it.

The judges now took their places in absolute silence at the side of the table facing me, and so I could recognize their faces. They were mostly the prelates who frequented the Cardinal's dinner table. Then the Cardinal himself entered and sat down on a pew-like elevated chair at the center of the table. The Censor of the Holly Office was missing, and I had the impression that the Cardinal had taken his place in order to conduct the trial. Contrary to my better judgement and reason I was filled with a desperate hope that he had assumed judicial authority in order to save my Master.

Two Dominican friars, also carrying lighted candles in their hands, now led my revered Master in and conducted him up to the middle of the unoccupied side of the table, so that he stood right in front of the crucifix and face to face with the Cardinal, whose countenance was illuminated by the mournful light from the smouldering candles. It was solemn, impenetrable, peculiarly withdrawn, just as at the end of our nocturnal conversation in the moonlight.

I had only caught sight of the Master's face for a moment as he was coming in. Now he was standing with his back to my box, and I noticed with grief that he was trembling.

The proceedings then began. A prayer invoking the Holy Spirit was recited. Then a Dominican friar at the other end of the table stood up and began reading out a document in Latin. It outlined the Master's work, or rather the condemnation of it. The constantly reiterated word "heresy, heresy" hit my ear with pitiless clarity. At last the reading was over. Now the individual judges delivered their pronouncements. Their voices were damped rather than carried by the uncanny silence of the hall. Finally the terrible word *"anathema"* passed from mouth to mouth, not flashed down majestically or angrily, but spoken indifferently, softly, coolly, like the murmur of a wave which rolls on, slowly washing over one person after another as if over dead cold pebbles on the beach.

The wave had rolled up to the Cardinal, and now it must surely break. Once more, against all reason and judgement, that desperate hope came over me! For here was the one person who had acknowledged the Master's teaching to be the truth, the one who towered high above the limitations of the age and who could change by his command the blindness of that age—the man who, like Peter, walked upon the waves.

But already the incomprehensible had happened: the wave had reached the Cardinal too. The same voice which a few nights before had admitted to me the Cardinal's conviction of the truth of the Master's views, now pronounced the word "anathema" over him. Peter, walking on the sea of the delusions of the time, had sunk in its waves. I clenched my fist in helpless rage. Accursed is the man who trusts his fellows, I thought. Now I saw the whole room as one great desolate sea of treachery. Only the crucifix still stood upright, but no one wanted to embrace it. And now the moment had surely come which Diana had thought of when she spoke of the fire with which they had burned Giordano Bruno, for now sentence would have to be passed.

Once more a voice rang through the cruel silence of the hall. The accused was offered the chance of pardon; he was invited to recant. Of course it was a mere formality.

During the condemnation of his teaching the Master had become more and more bent and dejected, but at the word "recant" he straightened up. Was it indignation? Ah, of course it could only be indignation! What a monstrous thought to imagine that he would destroy his true doctrine and his life's work!

But now I have to bear testimony for my Master—a great and painful testimony which, for good reasons, has been kept from the world up till now. For it was not as has been represented to a credulous world: that the revered Master had recanted his true teaching in fear and trembling in face of death and had himself made a deeply abject admission of his error. On the contrary, the Master recanted triumphantly, and there was no one present in the whole hall who did not understand that here was a man who would not show respect to his judges by disproving them, but would, as it were, repay their betrayal of the truth by his own betrayal of it. Was that the same man whom I had seen trembling on entering the hall? Was it possible that fear and trembling could change to presumption? Or were these two related in some mysterious way? Did the one produce the other when pushed to extremes? Where now was the devout and loyal Catholic whom I had so often praised to the Cardinal? Was he, by being driven to extremes, also changed to the opposite of what he had been? Had he fled to the extreme end of the possibility opened to him? I only know that I saw a man striding over his own personality as if it were a bit of unimportant matter. There was something incredibly sublime about his recantation; it expressed complete contempt for his judges and also contempt for his own person. And it was just this which lent to his recantation its shattering, indeed horrible grandeur. What disdain for his own self-destruction! The man surrendered completely, but over the fallen man the pride of the scientist rose, gloriously triumphant to the point of genuine arrogance. Did he give voice to it? Oh, no, he did not speak, but one could well imagine what he would have liked to say: *Yes, I am doing now just what you have done, I am betraying something which I hold to be true; I am betraying my science, but you are giving me freedom to confidently betray it! I know that at this moment I am unspeakably small, but my science is great and splendid! Whether you condemn it or I recant it,—and the one is as meaningless as the other—this scientific knowledge is unimpeachable and invincible. Even if I choke with shame here and now, I am willing to do so that my science may triumph in future times!*

And how did the judges take this most ambiguous of recantations? Ah, for me there was only one judge there! For what did I know, really, about those others who used to sit around the Cardinal's table and who were now assembled here? To what conclusion had they come or not come? The Cardinal alone stood clearly before my eyes, still as it were bathed in the spectral moonlight of our nocturnal conversation. I saw him sway on his high pew-like chair during the Master's recantation; I saw him, in his crimson robes, turning pale. Did the vision of the future and of man of the future rise up once more before his inner sight at that moment? Perhaps the man of the future was standing before him, and had become uncannily real just because they were trying to destroy him? And now precisely this man would have to be pardoned by him.

The Cardinal stood up heavily as though he had aged by many years in the interval. His resemblance to the Master was shattering: two men who each had overcome the man in himself stood face to face. Was it really the Cardinal who was beginning to speak now? Was not one really listening still to the voice of the other? Was there not in each word the same tremulous note of resistance against the sense of the words as in the Master's recantation of a few moments before? Pardon was spoken of, but deep distrust was meant; mercy was promised, but how unspeakably paltry it proved! Instead of being burned at the stake, to be under surveillance for one's whole life! And now the two candles on the judge's table slowly burned out. The gloomy room became even darker. The curtain fell. I seemed to hear the hours of future centuries striking. Two gates which up to now had stood open to each other, closed; two realms of the spirit rocked apart forever—and within me too.

I slipped away like a fugitive from the Palace of the Inquisition, overwhelmed with grief and horror, all my confidence and veneration shattered. Only one thing stood unshaken in the terrible collapse of my former world—the rejected truth. I loved it with defiance and joy precisely because it had been rejected. Never, never again would I enter the palace of the Cardinal who had abandoned it! But neither could I ever take my place again by the side of the Master, even if the Inquisition should set him free. Could a man who had once repudiated his doctrines, even if triumphantly, ever again represent that teaching worthily? Youth is incapable of compromise; for me the Master was silent for ever.

And now the moment came when at last I understood my beloved, who had foreseen the disastrous outcome from the beginning, and had herself been intimately connected in all that led up to it. I would live henceforth for the Master's work, as she had urgently begged me to do; I would lead the imprisoned knowledge into freedom; I would save and continue the interdicted work—but not here, surrounded by the Argus eyes of the Inquisition. True, my native Germany was closed to me owing to the great war, but there were other countries, the Northern lands, for instance, which the arms of persecution had not reached. I must get away somewhere, anywhere out of Rome!

I should have liked to leave the Eternal City that same day, for it would be no place in the future for even a pupil of the Master. But was not Diana also his pupil? And was not the Cardinal capable of delivering up his beloved niece to the Inquisition, not without sorrow, to be sure, but relentlessly trampling on his affections to do so? Certain of his utterances which I recalled from our conversation of that night now made me tremble with fear. Once more I was overcome with a consuming anxiety for my beloved. In any case I would have to see her again, to say good-bye and to explain my disappearance from Rome.

After some enquiries I found the home of her two chaperons and called on them. I was admitted at once, and now my worst fears were confirmed. Weeping, the ladies told me that Diana had not returned to them that evening after she rejected the Cardinal's plans for her marriage. The last veil concealing the state of things was now torn aside! The mystery of the Cardinal's litter, the drawn curtains, the hurried and furtive departure, my fruitless cries after her! Oh, my God, what had I allowed to happen to her by my unsuspecting nature! Where had my beloved been taken? The ladies were unable to give me any information; the Cardinal had only informed them that their protégée was staying in a convent of very strict observance, and that no one would be allowed to see her. I understood at once that this was a discreet way of getting an aristocratic lady who had apostatized out of the way and at the same time protecting her from herself. My first impulse was to storm all the convent gates in Rome, but then I felt how childishly hopeless this undertaking would be. The Cardinal did not stop at half measures; he demanded the utmost sacrifice from himself when it was a question of safeguarding the Faith and he demanded the same from others. I realized that I was up against the starkly inexorable.

So Diana's ardent wish to share her Master's fate was

fulfilled after all, even thought it was to be in this form of great and desolate abandonment. Now both symbolized the truth buried, perhaps forever. In my imagination I saw my beloved behind high trellised windows, surrounded by a quiet walled-in garden, where time ceases to exist. I saw her fading away in loneliness, like a beautiful noble flower. I knew that she was amenable to no comfort save that which came from her own strong soul in that outwardly unexpressed but inwardly profound communion with the beloved, for whom she willingly sacrificed herself without reward or thanks. A timorous, almost devout feeling of reverence came over me. No, I dare not free her even if I were able to! Had not her love always been fundamentally a love unto death? I must leave her to her destiny and fulfill mine. This fulfillment was the only love I could still show her. My decision to save the Master's interrupted work was also my final act of fidelity to her. I set off without hesitation.

Only when I was standing right in front of the Porta del Popolo did I notice that I was still wearing the Chaplain's cassock. There was no possibility of changing the garment now. I felt this false clothing to be a mockery, but after all it was affording me the right protection, at precisely the right moment?

On my way I came to one of Rome's many churches. Following a pious habit, I was about to enter for a moment to pray as usual for a blessing on my journey, but I hesitated on the threshold. What had I to seek here now? How could I desire a blessing for myself which had been so resolutely denied my scientific work? My spiritual home was no longer the Church, but the mighty new realm of the human mind; that was the threshold at which I now stood. And now a new self was born almost violently within me, rising up from the wreckage of my former life, a being unbound by conditions other than the law of free research —and without restraints from the spiritual world. Only what could be proved by science was valid for me now. The spiritual home in which I had lived up till now had been shattered, but I would build a new one for myself and for the rest of humanity, a brave and glorious home of freedom —and truth! I felt drunk with enthusiasm as I walked through the Porta del Popolo, away from the ostentatious façades of Rome's palaces, which for me concealed such terrible things; away from the loved girl for whom there was no longer any hope; out into the wild and lonely Campagna. Dusk was already falling; it would soon be dark. I was alone with Nature, the great unknown, oppressed by its enigmas and mysteries; I was a stranger in a strange country, and I was fleeing over unfamiliar and difficult roads. But the night wind, blowing over me from measureless distance, caressed my brow like a kiss of promise.

*

The document ended there. Even while the young scientist was reading the last lines the sirens suddenly started wailing outside. I sprang to my feet horrified but he firmly pushed me back on my chair. "That's only the preliminary warning; it doesn't concern us yet." And he read on calmly to the end.

The door suddenly burst open and the caretaker looked in. "The A.R.P. warning service announces the approach of a large flight," he said. "It may be dangerous for us tonight."

My young companion stood up. "Dangerous, did you say? They generally only fly over us." He stretched himself calmly. Then, with provoking indifference, he opened the door onto the balcony. "We mustn't miss the sight," he said. His composure enraged me, but it had a certain psychological influence: I followed him out more or less calmed.

The sirens had ceased wailing. The town lay beneath us in positively solemn silence, wrapped deeply in its protective blackout. The majestic dome of the night sky was arched over it; each single star shone intensely clear; the constellations shimmered enchantingly, like a floating silver veil.

I made an heroic effort to distract myself. "This is just like 'The Gate of Heaven' of our document," I said.

He looked at me with an ironical expression. "Yes," he replied, "that's what it looks like now at the Gate of Heaven—after a few centuries. But you'll soon see the difference!"

Now great white streaks of light commenced hurrying across the firmament as though invisible hands were feeling over the sky. "Those are searchlights looking for the enemy planes," said the young scientist. "Look! Now they've spotted what they've been searching for!" The two streaks of light suddenly joined together, then cut through each other and remained motionless in the sky, forming a huge cross. Down below the sirens started up again; they sounded horrible, like a wild beast howling up from an abyss. At the same moment some radiant pyramids of light appeared in the sky, and slowly floated down towards the town.

At this my companion's indifference changed in a flash to alertness. "Those are the enemy's Christmas trees," he cried. "Come! Let's get down to the cellar quickly. Christmas trees bring death!" He grabbed me by the hand and silently pulled me back into the house.

"Christmas trees bring death!" I repeated as I staggered in. "Christmas trees? What a blasphemy!"

We hurried down to the cellar where several people— the caretaker's family and some neighbors—had already gathered. I will pass over the hours which followed. I don't even know if they *were* hours. The terror of death cannot be measured by the hands of a clock. We were beyond the scope of time. We were outside the realm of man; we were in the hands of satanic powers. Oh, the horrible hissing sound of the bombs as they whizzed down; the appalling thundering bangs, as they fell! Yet what relief each time we realized that the bomb had not hit *us!* Then suddenly there was a mad yell from everyone, an unimaginable crashing and crackling, the rumble of falling stones; stifling clouds of dust, sepulchral darkness. Only at one single spot did some flickering light glimmer through a rent in the wall.

"Get out there!" ordered the young scientist. I crept through with the others, then staggered back to the depth of the cellar, for hell was loose outside! Then someone came behind me, I was seized, pulled, dragged, and pushed out on to the street, which was a sea of billowing, dancing flames. So this was the terrible carnival for which the town had masked itself! Again I tried to turn back to the cellar; again I felt the harsh relentless grip of my companion.

"Get on!" he shouted. Feeling desperate, but irresolutely obedient like a small child, I ran through the surging alley of flames into the street where house after house was burning.

And now you will ask about the documents which I had come to the town to save. Of course we had taken them with us down to the cellar—I remember well how the young man put the case full of the family documents down on the ground beside me, while I held clutched in my hand the paper he had just read to me. I was still holding it pressed against me when I crept through the cleft in the wall. But then when I caught sight of the burning street, well, I simply tossed it away. The breath of the fire caught the pages and whirled them away. I saw them blazing, but that didn't worry me then.

Also later on, long after we had been saved, I felt no regret nor even surprise about it. Things had simply happened just as I had foreseen that they would on arriving in the blacked-out town. Now the unmasking was taking place after that terrible carnival. Not only the document was revealed as valueless but with it everything else which up to now had given purpose and direction to my life. I felt strangely poor and despoiled.

All the things which I had hitherto regarded as permanently valid values—humanity and Christianity, rank and culture, position and tradition—all these things were suddenly as if they had never been. Or, if they ever had been, they were finally denuded of their meaning, and with it the meaning and purpose of the life I had lived with such confidence. My own era had gone under. Where did I belong now?

My cousin Marianne, who remained with me at first with her children, had no understanding at all for my feelings: it was simply that she had not been through that night of bombs. While I, in my undisturbed rural domesticity, was mourning things lost which could never be restored, she, who had actually lost her home, was already happily planning the replacement of what had been destroyed and looking forward to the pleasant task of buying new things. In short, she was convinced that everything would soon be exactly as it had been before. No, not quite everything! The loss of the family archives seemed to strike the only discordant note in this mental harmony of hers. Of course she was far too tactful and kind to reproach me, but she could not forgive herself for not having gone to the town to fetch the documents herself. However, she comforted herself with the reflection that the genealogical tree and the most important events in the family history could perhaps be collected again from old church registers and historical records.

But as for the so-called "Galilean Document," which she valued so much, no clue to it survived anywhere except in the memories of those who had read it with such rapt attention. She therefore decided to reconstruct this document herself, and as I myself was not so enthusiastic about the matter, feeling as I did at the time, she invited her young cousin, who had read the document to me that night of the blitz, to come and stay with her. After the collapse of the German front, we learned to our great surprise that he had not been taken prisoner as Marianne's husband had, but had been given a favorable offer to go abroad, which assured him the chance of continuing his scientific studies. He wrote that he would come to say good-bye to us before leaving.

So this tall slim young man arrived at my house one day. His clear-cut features still bore the somewhat superior, slightly strained expression which I had found so irritating and disquieting at one time. In the interval he had saved my life—for I myself would never have had the courage to leave the cellar and rush into the flaming street that night. Of course it was only natural that I should remind him of this once more. He laughed outright. "Yes," he said, "you'll turn up again as my lucky number, the only one I have to show for that time."

"You talk as if you were normally a barbarian," said Marianne jocosely, "and yet even during the war you only worked in a laboratory."

"That's just it. That was the proper den of murderers," he replied somewhat cryptically, "but let's not talk about it." He looked around my house with interest. "So you've still got all your old-fashioned stuff here."

"Do you not find it comforting after the bombed town?" asked Marianne.

"To be quite honest, ruins have their good side too," he said. "They let a breath of fresh air into a stuffy old house."

"Stuffy old house?" repeated Marianne disapprovingly. "Tell me, what *are* you talking about?"

Now he laughed again. He still had a somewhat challenging attitude and a youthfully flippant way of speaking to the older generation, but I did not feel annoyed by this as I used to! Was it that I, having become somewhat estranged from my own generation, had thereby come closer to his? I found something liberating in his presence as though he had to help me even today out of the darkness as in that night of blitz. In a word, I scented the new life in him.

Marianne now began to talk about the document, and urged him to help us by telling what he could remember. "I'm so glad that you read it that last night," she said, "because now you know how frightfully important it was."

He didn't show any special enthusiasm. Yes, he had read

the thing, he said, but he did not find it particularly interesting. Nowadays the Inquisition would not find it necessary to get all worked up about the Master's teaching.

Marianne looked at him wide-eyed. "What do you mean?" she asked innocently.

"I mean that nowadays our scientists could simply say to the Cardinal: Your Eminence, we scientists are not in a position to determine even the center of the universe, in a manner which would suit the theologians."

"But surely that's quite impossible," cried Marianne indignantly. "At that rate all the centuries of struggle would have been in vain!"

"They were right in their day," he admitted, "and of course they have left us several systems, but when all is said and done everything is relative. . . ."

She shook her head vehemently. Of course she didn't believe a word of it. How should she? We had both been brought up in an attitude of reverent faith in the infallibility of science.

She turned to me. "Do help me," she cried impetuously. "What this disrespectful young man says can't be true. I think he doesn't take us seriously."

"Yes, it may well be true, Marianne," I said. "In that night of blitz it came home to me very clearly that everything—yes, absolutely everything which we have and which we are is transitory."

She was visibly dismayed at this. "But at that rate," she said hesitantly, "at that rate the trial of the Master was quite senseless and also the fate of poor Diana and her friend—then the Church must have been terribly wrong in condemning them without any reason. . . ."

But now the discussion took a quite unexpected turn. "Damn it all, you're wrong there! There was sense in what the Church tried to do that time," cried the young scientist. "I don't mean the methods of the Inquisition, I mean the Cardinal's vision—for *it* was quite correct! That man knew human nature. He knew three hundred years ago exactly how it would be with us today. The Diana of the document could still say: 'There are only the eternal laws and we human beings.' Today there are neither the eternal laws nor human beings."

"But after all we do believe in what is good, and we're Christians," stammered Marianne.

"Indeed? *Are* we still Christians?" he asked. "That's very interesting. Certainly one would never notice it, and I thought it was clearly disproved by this war of bombing. Nevertheless, it doesn't seem to have been enough to convince you people here. But just you wait! Hiroshima will soon be far surpassed!"

At that moment one of Marianne's children began crying loudly in the next room and she went out to see what was the matter. The young man and I were left alone for a few minutes.

I had grasped what he meant. The word "Hiroshima" had struck me like a flash of lightning. "You mustn't go abroad," I said. "You mustn't help on those terrible developments of science."

His strenuous face had an expression of intense perception. "I see that you know what I shall be doing abroad," he said, "but it's too late to change my mind. And not only because I've already agreed to go. After all, what good would it be if I were to remain here? Others would follow the call instead of me. Am I to hand over my opportunities to them? In any case the inventions will go on developing: no one and nothing can hinder the progress of science.

He stated this as a certainty with apparent unconcern, but his words no longer deceived me. Suddenly our relations towards each other were reversed. I now felt a sense of superiority towards him which really shattered me. The extraordinary, almost touching disparity between his deficient human development and the high degree of specialized scientific knowledge which he undoubtedly possessed struck me very forcibly for the first time. His youth was a mute appeal—my God, as far as age was concerned I could have been his mother! And now it was up to me to help him, but I didn't know how to.

"But when you scientists discover more and more new things in your science, does it never occur to you that there could also be a God?" I cried desperately.

"Oh, yes," he replied calmly, "that idea does actually come to us. After a long, long time we are beginning to think in terms of God again. For, you see, it has become rather difficult to explain the universe without a Creator. But it's not easy for us to take Him in, we've lived too long without Him. After all, we had to. Remember the 'Galilean

Document'! You probably know more about God than I do."

Alas, no, I really didn't know much about Him either—He had never played an important part in my life, and I had not even felt this as a loss. For of course we had all gone to Church, we had belonged to Christian societies and given gifts to the poor at Christmas. But now even that scanty relationship with God was to be counted in the long list of losses sustained in that night of bombing. In vain I sought an answer to give my young friend, but Marianne had come back and the three of us set to work making notes about the lost document.

*

It was late in the night when the young man at last took leave of us. Marianne had said good-bye to him in the drawing room and gone back to her children as one of them had started crying in his sleep again, so I accompanied the guest to his car. We walked across the lawn in silence. To night too the stars were shining gloriously as they had once shone over Diana and her young friend up in the Gate of Heaven. In the heavens the span of time since then was only a fleeting moment. Up there all our interpretations and misinterpretations were nothing more than meteors which flamed up, then died down. But here below on earth poor humanity was stumbling and falling.

Now he was starting up the engine, in a few minutes he would be gone. And what were my last words to him to be? He had saved my life, and now he was going abroad to help destroy life. Was not he an example of mankind wavering between humanity and inhumanity, and was not I a mirror of man's utter helplessness?

"You're very silent! Are you still thinking about God?" he asked casually.

I had to decide on something to say. "I'm thinking how frightened Diana was that time up in the Gate of Heaven because God was no longer to be found in the universe, and I believe that you people today are frightened that you may find Him again."

He hesitated for a moment before answering, then he suddenly changed his tone—it was for the first time. Had this tone been only a kind of mask too? The last mask fell from him. "Yes," he said frankly, "perhaps you're right. We're afraid, because everywhere we're standing at the last frontiers, and if we were to find our way back to God again, we could no longer include Him in our laws of causality. Then He'd be a God who would really have something to say. But that time hasn't come yet, so let's make the best of our freedom!"

He shook hands in a comradely way, started up his car, and drove off.

I stood there looking after him until the last sound had died away. Yes, God must have something to say again, to me too. Fundamentally, we were all faced with the same decision. What would it turn out to be?